OUR COSMOS

THE COMPLETE GUIDE TO SPACE FOR KIDS

PROFESSOR RAMAN PRINJA

ILLUSTRATED BY **SUZIE MASON**

To Kamini, Vikas, and Sachin—R.P.
For Richard and Rupert, for always—S.M.

Published in 2024 by Welbeck Editions
An Imprint of Hachette Children's Books,
Part of Hodder & Stoughton Limited
Carmelite House, 50 Victoria Embankment
London EC4Y 0DZ

An Hachette UK Company
www.hachette.co.uk
www.hachettechildrens.co.uk

A CIP catalogue record for this book is available from the British Library and
The Library of Congress.

HB ISBN: 978-1-803-38131-2
Ebook ISBN: 978-1-803-38141-1 (UK only)

Printed in China

10 9 8 7 6 5 4 3 2 1

MIX
Paper | Supporting
responsible forestry
FSC® C104740
FSC
www.fsc.org

OUR COSMOS

THE COMPLETE GUIDE TO SPACE FOR KIDS

PROFESSOR RAMAN PRINJA

ILLUSTRATED BY **SUZIE MASON**

CONTENTS

EXPLORING THE UNIVERSE

The universe is exciting, enormous, and it is expanding. All living things, and every star, planet, moon, and galaxy, is part of the universe. It also includes energy, time, and space.

Scientists explain how the universe began by using the idea of a big bang. In this idea, the universe started from just a single tiny point about 13.8 billion years ago (that makes it 13,800,000,000 years old!). Over this great age, the universe has stretched and expanded to become as enormous as it is today. And it's still growing.

Astronomers are scientists who study the universe. Their studies have shown that the universe has more than 200 billion galaxies that can be seen. Each of these galaxies is made up of billions of stars. In total, there are septillion stars in the universe, which is written as the number 1 followed by 24 zeros!

Exploring the universe is like opening different doors and finding amazing objects and great mysteries behind each one. In this book, we're going to discover what's behind some incredible space doors!

LIGHT-YEARS APART

As you explore the universe in this book, your imagination will be stretched, and no more so than in grasping the vastness of space. You may think traveling hundreds of miles between cities is a long journey or that flying abroad on vacation is a long-distance adventure. But these distances, and even the scale of the Earth, are really tiny compared to the size of the solar system, galaxies, and the whole cosmos.

Mercury

Venus

Earth

Mars

Jupiter

IMAGINARY ROAD TRIPS

Let's go on some imaginary road trips. If you were to complete one lap around the Earth's equator, traveling in a car moving at 62 miles per hour [mph] (100 kilometers per hour [kph]), the journey would take more than 17 days. Now let's pretend there was a 240,000-mile (385,000-km) road to the Moon. Traveling nonstop, our car would take six months to reach it! Still driving at 62 mph (100 kph), our sturdy car would take about 177 years to go from the Earth to the Sun and more than 5,000 years to reach the outermost planet, Neptune. And that's just a road trip in the solar system! There are still billions of other stars in our galaxy and trillions of other galaxies in the universe to explore!

LIGHT-YEARS AWAY

Using everyday measurements of distance such as feet, miles, meters, and kilometers is not very useful when we look at the enormous scale of the universe, since these numbers become extremely large to write. For example, the distance to the star Alpha Centauri would be written as 24,854,847,689,493 miles (40,000,000,000,000 km)!

In astronomy, we use a different unit of distance instead, called a light-year. Light zips through empty space at a speed of 186,400 miles per second [mps] (300,000 kilometers per second [kps]). At this speed, it takes just eight minutes to travel the 93 million miles (150 million km) distance between the Sun and Earth. However, light takes 4.3 years to travel the distance from Alpha Centauri to us, so we can say that Alpha Centauri is 4.3 light-years away.

Our Milky Way galaxy is 100,000 light-years in diameter, meaning that light would take 100,000 years to travel from one end of the galaxy to the other. Astronomers estimate that the universe that we can see in telescopes is 93 billion light-years across.

Saturn

Uranus

Neptune

LOOKING BACK IN TIME

The night sky is like a cosmic time machine. When we look at objects that are very far away, the light hitting us from them will have started traveling from the object a long time ago. This means that we are not seeing what the object looks like now, but rather what it looked like some time ago, when the light was first emitted.

Since light takes eight minutes to reach us from the Sun, when we safely view the Sun we are really seeing it as it was eight minutes ago. A galaxy called NGC 4845 is about 65 million light-years away. We are seeing it in our telescopes as it was 65 million years ago. This means that the light that we see left NGC 4845 around the time dinosaurs became extinct on Earth!

TIMELINE OF THE UNIVERSE

The universe has a history that goes back billions of years. Scientists use math, astronomy, and physics to work out what it was like in the past. By understanding how forces such as gravity work, and by looking at stars and galaxies in space, scientists can work out a timeline of events in the life of the universe.

COSMIC TIMELINE

Most scientists believe that the universe began about 13.8 billion years ago with an event called the big bang. The big bang was not an explosion; instead, it was space appearing EVERYWHERE. The universe started in a single point that was incredibly hot and everything was very tightly squeezed together (or dense). It then had a rapid growth spurt! The universe started to expand, and as it got larger, it also got cooler and less tightly packed. It has expanded and cooled ever since.

100 to 1,000 seconds after the big bang, light elements such as hydrogen and helium are made.

A few million years after the big bang, clumps of gas come together under gravity to make the first stars.

300,000 years later, the first light (or radiation) is released by the universe, which we can still detect today as a faint glow.

It was only about 240 million years ago that the first dinosaurs walked the Earth.

A few billion years later, galaxies are formed. Meanwhile, the universe is starting to grow at a faster rate because of a mysterious force known as dark energy.

The first humans appeared 200,000 year ago, and the first human civilization formed around 12,000 years ago.

9 billion years after the big bang, the Sun, planets, and the rest of the solar system is formed. Soon after the Earth is made, the first simple types of life appear on our planet.

You can see from this cosmic timeline that the length of time that humans have been around is very tiny compared to the great 13.8-billion-year history of the universe!

ANCIENT ASTRONOMY

Ancient civilizations watched the night sky and the movements of the Sun, Moon, and planets. Some believed they were watching their gods that ruled over day and night or the seasons. To help them understand the meaning of these movements, ancient civilizations built amazing structures in many parts of the world. Our ancestors used them to learn and predict the positions of the Sun, Moon, and stars. This meant that they could keep time, decide when to farm and harvest, and find their way when traveling at night.

STONEHENGE

Stonehenge in Wiltshire, England, is one of the most famous prehistoric stone monuments in the world. It was built somewhere between 5000 BCE and 1520 BCE and was originally made up of an outer circle of 30 precisely placed stones called sarsens. There were also smaller outer circles and five giant arches. Some of the stones still standing today are almost 23 feet [ft] (7 meters [m]) tall.

Stonehenge may have been used for worship and healing. It was also used as a site for ancient astronomy. It has a carefully placed Heel Stone, which is lined up so that the Sun always rises over it on the longest day of the year. This day marks the summer solstice—the first day of summer. In the winter, the shortest day of the year is also marked by the way the Sun rises and sets between the giant stones.

CHICHÉN ITZÁ

The ancient Maya civilization in South America had many expert stargazers who made very careful studies of the motions of stars and planets. Their city of Chichén Itzá in today's Mexico was built in the seventh century and has a 79-ft- (24-m-) high pyramid at its center, with four stairways around its outside.

Chichén Itzá was built to mark the spring and fall (autumn) equinoxes. These are special times of the year when the length of the day and night are equal. When the Sun sets on these equinox days, a shadow is cast on the north-facing stairway that looks like a snake slithering downward!

CHEOMSEONGDAE

Dating back to the seventh century, there is a tower in South Korea that is thought be the oldest astronomical observatory in Asia. Known as Cheomseongdae, it is made of 365 pieces of granite, which were placed in 27 circular layers to make a 31-ft- (9.4-m-) tall tower. It has a window that ancient astronomers peered through to get clear views of the night sky.

PICTURES IN THE SKY

For many centuries past, our ancient ancestors were fascinated by the stars in the night sky. They connected together groups of stars to form patterns that looked like gods, animals, and heroes from their cultures. These imaginary pictures in the sky were used to tell wonderful stories that have been passed down through the generations by African, Asian, Greek, Roman, Native North American, and many other cultures.

A JIGSAW OF CONSTELLATIONS

Today, we recognize these imaginary pictures as 88 official constellations. Together, they fit like pieces of a jigsaw puzzle to fill the entire sky. The constellations you can see depend on the time of the year. Our view into space changes as the Earth is in motion and orbiting around the Sun, and the sky looks slightly different each night as the Earth glides to a different spot in its orbit.

Where you live on Earth also affects the constellations than you can see. The northern hemisphere is always pointing in a different direction to the southern hemisphere. This means that stargazers in Europe, for example, get a different view of the night sky and can see different constellations than those in South Africa.

GUIDED BY THE SKY

Constellations have been known for centuries and were not just used by ancient cultures to tell amazing stories. Because constellations are in a fixed location in the sky, they can be used as signposts. Bright stars in well-known constellations can be used to navigate. Sailors used the stars like a compass, following the constellations as they journeyed across oceans to discover new lands.

Constellations were also used by ancient farmers as clocks. By spotting different constellations through the seasons, farmers made decisions on when to plant and when to harvest. Astronomers still use constellations today to name stars and meteor showers. For example, the brightest star in the constellation of Leo (the Lion) is Alpha Leonis.

Gazing into a dark star-filled night sky is a wonderful experience. Try to trace famous constellations, and share the myths and great legends that our ancestors spoke of. It's a fun way to start exploring the universe!

NORTHERN HEMISPHERE: WINTER CONSTELLATIONS

Winter in the northern hemisphere is a great time to pick out bright stars and some very well-known constellations in the night sky. The nights get dark early, so you don't have to be up late to have fun with star-hopping. Wrap up warm, though—the skies are amazing on crystal clear nights, but these perfect stargazing conditions also mean it is likely to be very cold! Here are some famous constellations to pick out.

ORION: THE HUNTER

One of the easiest constellations to recognize is Orion, named after the great hunter in ancient Greek mythology. Look for it after 9 p.m. in January or February. To find Orion, look for three medium bright stars in a short, straight row—they mark the belt around the hunter's waistline. Then pick out two even brighter stars. The reddish one is named Betelgeuse, and it marks one of Orion's shoulders. The other bright star, known as Rigel, is blue, and it marks the left leg of the hunter.

On very dark evenings, you might notice three faint stars dropping in a line below the Orion's belt. These stars trace a sword. A fuzzy patch at the sword's center is a beautiful star-making factory known as the Orion nebula.

Betelgeuse

Rigel

TAURUS: THE BULL

Using Orion's belt as a good starting point, if you gaze upward and to the right of Orion's shoulder, you'll head to another easy-to-spot constellation named Taurus. A V-shape pattern of stars trace the horns of the bull, which seems to be charging toward Orion! Look for a bright reddish-orange star named Aldebaran, which marks out one of the bull's eyes.

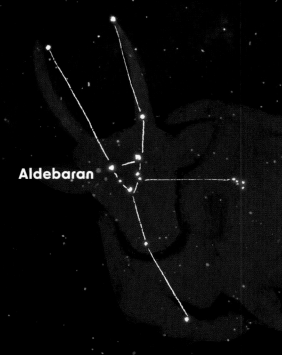

Aldebaran

CASSIOPEIA: THE QUEEN

Seen during late winter and spring evenings in the northern hemisphere, Cassiopeia is a lovely constellation found toward the northwest sky. Its five main stars draw out the shape of the letter "M" or "W." In ancient Greek myths, these stars were described as the throne upon which Queen Cassiopeia sits.

The Big Dipper

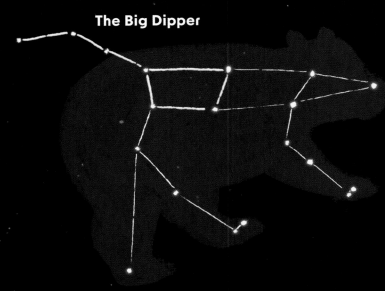

URSA MAJOR: THE GREAT BEAR

Ursa Major is the largest constellation in the northern hemisphere. Within it is a famous grouping named the Big Dipper, also known as the Plough. Six of the seven stars of the Big Dipper are the brightest stars in this constellation. A great sight using a good telescope is a pair of galaxies named Messier 81 and Messier 82—they can be found just above the Great Bear's head.

NORTHERN HEMISPHERE: SUMMER CONSTELLATIONS

Summer may bring shorter nights and later sunsets, but you can take advantage of the warmer weather to spend more time outside, searching the star-studded night sky. Some of the easy-to-recognize constellations and favorite cosmic objects are on view at this time of the year.

LYRA: THE LYRE

It may be one of the smallest constellations, but Lyra has an important place in the summer night sky. Best seen during August, it is home to Vega, the fifth brightest star in the entire night sky. Vega is the brightest star in a famous pattern known as the Summer Triangle, which is made by joining lines between this star, Deneb (in the constellation of Cygnus), and Altair (in the constellation of Aquila).

RING NEBULA (LYRA)

Located in Lyra and a beautiful sight when viewed through a telescope, the Ring Nebula is the glowing remains of a dying Sun-like star that has puffed away its outer layers. The nebula lies about 2,000 light-years away from Earth.

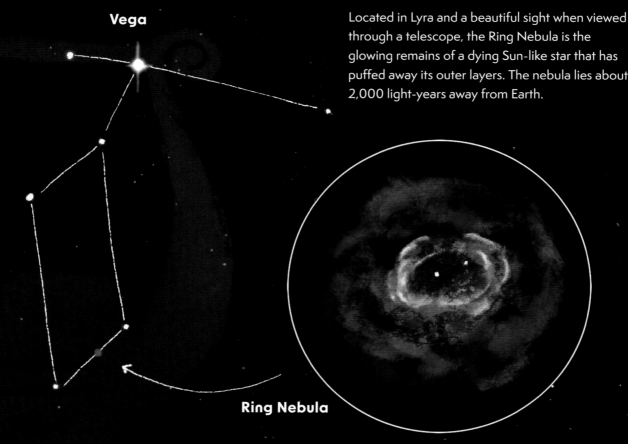

Vega

Ring Nebula

CYGNUS: THE SWAN

During September, look for the beautiful sight of 10 bright stars drawing out the shape of a swan with outstretched wings. Cygnus' four brightest stars—Deneb, Albireo, Gienah, and Sàdr—form an easily picked-out shape within Cygnus named the Northern Cross.

This constellation is home to an amazing object known as Cygnus X-1. It is a black hole around 6,000 light-years away from Earth and about fifteen times the mass of the Sun. The black hole is orbited by a massive blue star.

Albireo

Sadr

Deneb   Gienah

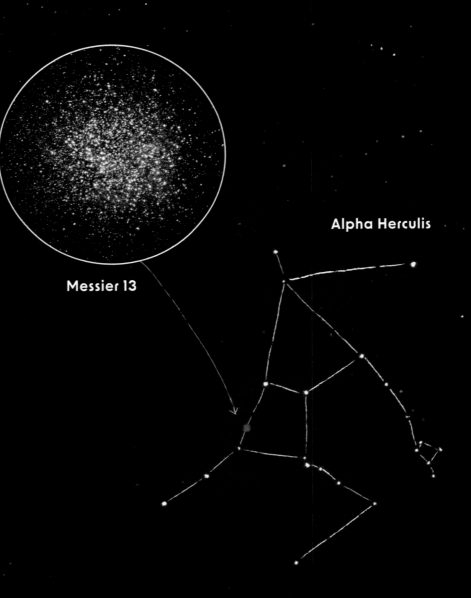

Messier 13

Alpha Herculis

HERCULES: THE HERO

The constellation of Hercules is named after a hero from Roman mythology who has superhuman strength. This large constellation is best viewed during July. Its brightest stars trace the shape of a manlike figure, with its brightest star marking the hero's head.

MESSIER 13 (HERCULES)

A highlight within this constellation is an object named Messier 13 (M13). Viewed using small telescopes, M13 is revealed as a tight group or cluster of around 300,000 stars!

SOUTHERN HEMISPHERE CONSTELLATIONS

Not all constellations are visible from one point on Earth. Some stars are best seen from the half of the Earth that is south of the equator. Most of the constellations in the sky of the southern hemisphere were devised between the sixteenth and nineteenth century by sailors exploring East Asia. Many were named after animals the explorers had seen on their journeys, while others were named after scientific instruments that they used to navigate the seas.

CRUX: SOUTHERN CROSS

One of the most famous and easily recognizable southern constellations is Crux (or Southern Cross). It is the smallest of the 88 constellations, made up of just four stars. Crux is also well-known for its appearance on the national flags of five different countries: Brazil, Samoa, Papua New Guinea, New Zealand, and Australia.

CARINA: THE KEEL

The stars of the constellation Carina trace the shape of the bottom of a mythical ship named *Argo*. Its brightest star is Canopus, and it is the second-brightest star in the sky. A highlight found in Carina is a very unstable, powerful star named Eta Carinae. It is a hundred times more massive than the Sun, and astronomers believe it will explode as a supernova over the next few million years.

Eta Carinae

Canopus

CENTAURUS: THE CENTAUR

Visible throughout March in the southern sky, Centaurus is the ninth-largest constellation. In ancient Greek mythology, Centaurs were beasts that were half human and half horse. The band of the Milky Way passes through Centaurus, making it a very interesting part of the sky to explore. The nearest star to Earth (after the Sun), Proxima Centauri, is found in this constellation, some 4.3 light-years away.

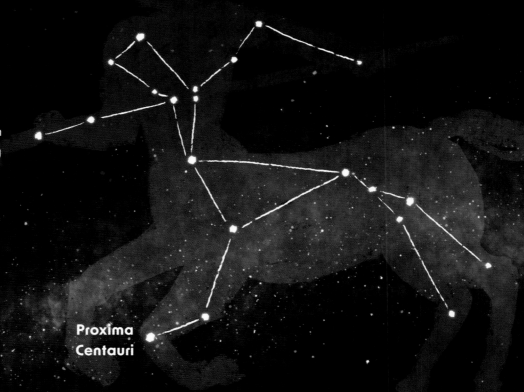

Proxima Centauri

Gliese 667Cc

Antares

SCORPIUS: THE SCORPION

The southern skies present excellent views of Scorpius. Looking high up, the shape of a scorpion is fairly easy to make out, with the bright star Antares marking its head. The scorpion's curving tail is traced by a string of bright stars.

A few stars in Scorpius are exciting because of the planets (known as exoplanets) that orbit around them. Gliese 667Cc is a "super-Earth" roughly four times the size of Earth. It orbits a red dwarf star named Gliese 667C in Scorpius, only 22 light-years away from Earth.

ALL THE LIGHT

When we look up at the stars in the night sky, we see the light from very distant planets, stars, and galaxies. Light is very important for all the discoveries we make about the cosmos. Astronomers gather light in telescopes and study it carefully to learn about the objects in space. However, the light we see with our eyes is just a tiny part of the full range of light that's known as the electromagnetic spectrum.

THE ELECTROMAGNETIC SPECTRUM

The full range of the electromagnetic spectrum is made of radio waves, microwaves, infrared, visual (or optical), ultraviolet, X-rays, and gamma rays. Light behaves like a wave, and as with all waves, it has peaks and dips. The distance between two peaks is called a wavelength. The parts of the electromagnetic spectrum have light of different wavelengths.

ULTRAVIOLET

Ultraviolet light is the part of the electromagnetic spectrum that gives us sunburn. In space, it is given off by objects that give out a lot of energy, such as very massive stars.

X-RAYS

With a wavelength that measures about the size of an atom, X-rays are used in hospitals because they can go through skin and muscle to take photos of bones. Explosions from the Sun and other superhot gases in space give off X-rays.

GAMMA RAYS

The most energetic objects in the universe put out gamma rays. They can be detected coming from very massive stars that have exploded at the end of their lives.

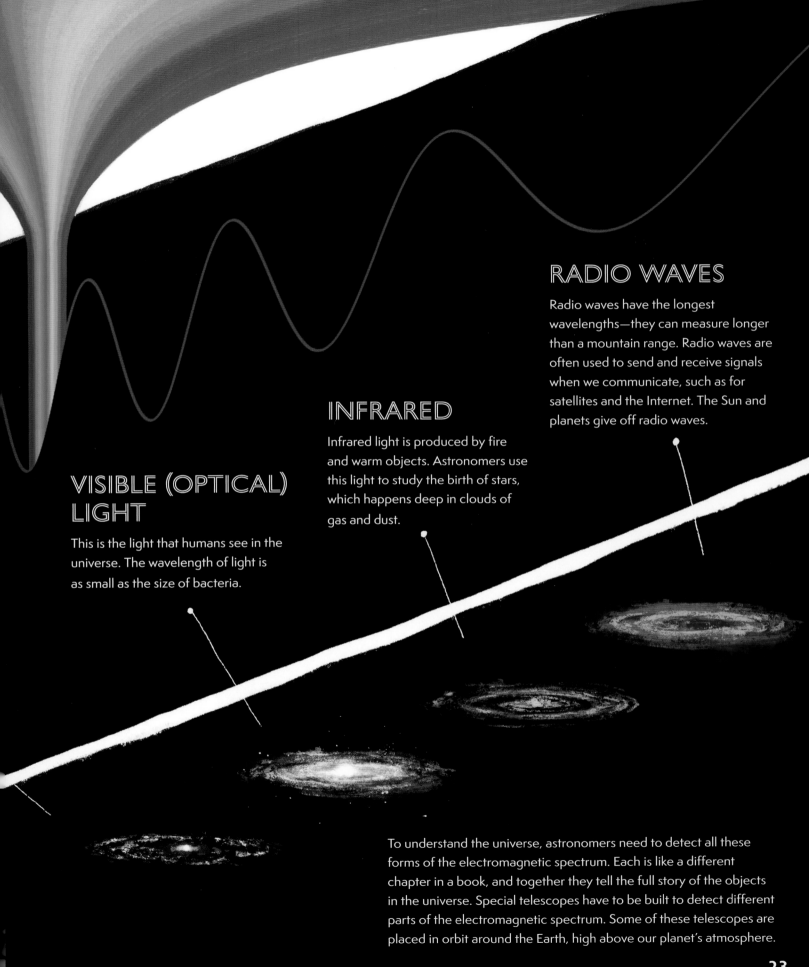

RADIO WAVES

Radio waves have the longest wavelengths—they can measure longer than a mountain range. Radio waves are often used to send and receive signals when we communicate, such as for satellites and the Internet. The Sun and planets give off radio waves.

INFRARED

Infrared light is produced by fire and warm objects. Astronomers use this light to study the birth of stars, which happens deep in clouds of gas and dust.

VISIBLE (OPTICAL) LIGHT

This is the light that humans see in the universe. The wavelength of light is as small as the size of bacteria.

To understand the universe, astronomers need to detect all these forms of the electromagnetic spectrum. Each is like a different chapter in a book, and together they tell the full story of the objects in the universe. Special telescopes have to be built to detect different parts of the electromagnetic spectrum. Some of these telescopes are placed in orbit around the Earth, high above our planet's atmosphere.

EYES ON THE UNIVERSE

Telescopes are the most important scientific tool used in astronomy, and they have entirely changed our understanding of the universe. Since the earliest invented telescopes were pointed toward the sky more than 400 years ago, they have become larger and more powerful.

COLLECTING LIGHT

Telescopes are important because they improve our views and make distant objects appear closer. The pupils of our eyes are a fraction of an inch across and can only collect light over a tiny area. Telescopes can be many feet or meters wide, so they have a huge area to collect lots of light. You can think of them as buckets that collect light! They allow us to see more of the objects that are very far away, and they enable us to examine finer details on nearby stars and planets. Telescopes can also be built to detect other parts of the electromagnetic spectrum, including X-rays and ultraviolet rays.

TYPES OF TELESCOPES

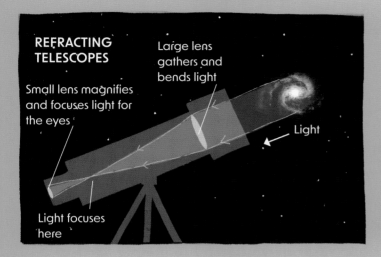

REFRACTING TELESCOPES

Small lens magnifies and focuses light for the eyes

Large lens gathers and bends light

Light focuses here

Light

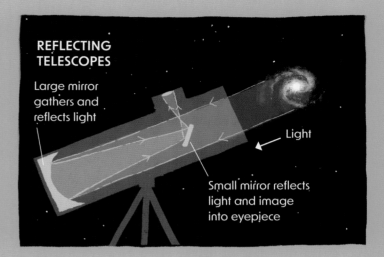

REFLECTING TELESCOPES

Large mirror gathers and reflects light

Small mirror reflects light and image into eyepiece

Light

Telescopes that use lenses are called refracting telescopes. The lenses bend the light and magnify the object to make it look bigger and closer than it actually is. The telescope that Galileo Galilei used in the 1600s was a refracting telescope. To see far into the universe, you need a very big, powerful lens, but this type of lens is very heavy, making the telescope difficult to move around.

Telescopes that use mirrors are called reflecting telescopes. Unlike a lens, a mirror can be made very thin, so even a large one will not be too heavy. The mirrors are carefully shaped and polished to gather and focus the light. Professional astronomers today use reflecting telescopes that can have many mirrors perfectly fixed together to act like a single mirror of 33 ft (10 m) wide or more!

GALILEO GALILEI

In the early 1600s, the Italian astronomer Galileo Galilei was one of the first people to use a telescope in astronomy. His telescope was less than 1 inch [in] (3 centimeters [cm]) in diameter and just 4.3 ft (1.3 m) long, but he made some startling discoveries with it in the skies around him. With this simple telescope made of small lenses, Galileo studied the Moon and discovered the four largest moons of Jupiter. He also made the observation that Saturn had lobes, or "ears," on either side. These were later identified as Saturn's rings by Christian Huygens in 1665.

One of a series of Moon sketches drawn by Galileo

OBSERVATORIES ON EARTH

A building that houses large telescopes and other scientific equipment is called an observatory. It will usually have a dome-shaped roof, with an opening for pointing the telescope out to the sky. The location of an observatory is carefully selected by astronomers. They are often built in remote locations, far from the glare of city lights, and in areas that have mainly dry weather with fewer clouds. The observatories on Earth are mainly used to detect the visible and infrared light of the electromagnetic spectrum.

MAUNA KEA

Some of the most powerful observatories on Earth are located 13,800 ft (4,200 m) high on the dormant volcano Mauna Kea, on the island of Hawaii. This site is home to over 12 telescopes, and they are used by astronomers from many countries. The collection includes a twin pair called the Keck Telescopes—each has a mirror measuring 33 ft (10 m) in diameter.

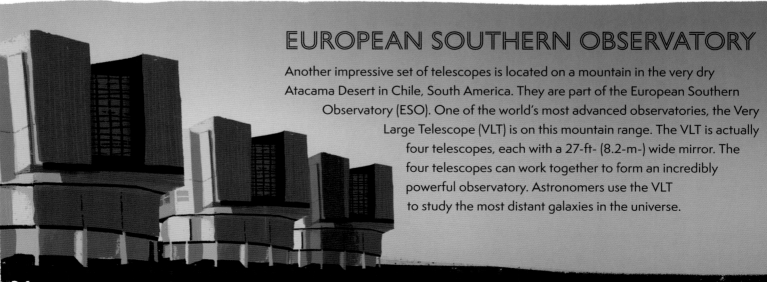

EUROPEAN SOUTHERN OBSERVATORY

Another impressive set of telescopes is located on a mountain in the very dry Atacama Desert in Chile, South America. They are part of the European Southern Observatory (ESO). One of the world's most advanced observatories, the Very Large Telescope (VLT) is on this mountain range. The VLT is actually four telescopes, each with a 27-ft- (8.2-m-) wide mirror. The four telescopes can work together to form an incredibly powerful observatory. Astronomers use the VLT to study the most distant galaxies in the universe.

LA PALMA

The Canary Islands are a popular vacation destination located off the west coast of Africa. One of the islands, formed by an volcano, is La Palma. It rises some 7,900 ft (2,400 m) above the Atlantic Ocean and is the site of more than 20 observatories. Astronomers come from all over the world to use the telescopes here.

SALT

Located in South Africa, SALT is the largest optical telescope in the Southern Hemisphere. Its main mirror is 36 ft (11 m) in diameter, and it is actually 91 small hexagonal pieces that fit perfectly together to work like one giant mirror. The SALT telescope can detect stars billions of times dimmer than the faintest stars that can be seen with the human eye alone!

RADIO ASTRONOMY

Astronomers also use telescopes that can detect radio waves coming from stars, planets, and galaxies. The radio part of the electromagnetic spectrum can also come from cold, dark clouds of gas and dust in space that do not put out any visible light. Radio waves coming from objects in the universe are very weak, sometimes a million times less powerful than the signal from a cell phone (mobile phone)! Special radio telescopes have to be built to detect the very faintest of signals.

RADIO TELESCOPES

A radio telescope usually has three main parts. There is an antenna to collect the radio waves—these are usually bowl-shaped dishes made of metal, with diameters as large as 164 ft (50 m) across. The radio telescope will also have a receiver and an amplifier to boost the very weak signal. Since radio waves have long wavelengths, they are not blocked out by clouds. This means that radio telescopes can be used in cloudy skies as well as in daylight.

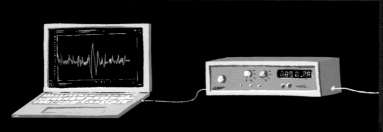

Signals are sent from the telescope to the receiver and amplifier (shown on the right) and transferred to a computer for processing.

VERY LARGE ARRAY

Often, many radio astronomy dishes are connected together to create a superpowerful telescope. One example of this is the Very Large Array (VLA). This incredible radio telescope is located in New Mexico, USA, and has 27 huge dishes, each measuring 82 ft (25 m) in diameter. By linking them together and combining their signal, astronomers have made an enormous telescope that spreads over 22 miles (35 km) in the desert! They are studying radio signals from the center of our Milky Way galaxy.

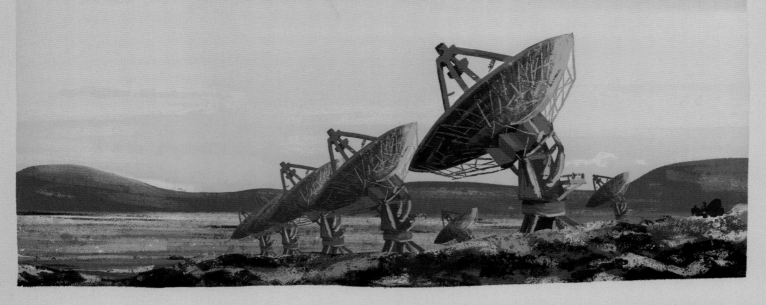

SQUARE KILOMETRE ARRAY

Scientists and engineers from more than 20 countries are working together to build the world's most powerful radio telescope. It is named the Square Kilometre Array (SKA), and when it is fully completed in 2030, it will link together thousands of radio dishes. Located in remote parts of South Africa and Australia, the SKA will help astronomers to understand some of the great mysteries of the universe. Very excitingly, they will be looking for the faintest signals from the first stars and galaxies that were made when the universe started with a big bang. The SKA will also teach us about how galaxies change in time—and how the universe itself is ever expanding.

TELESCOPES IN SPACE

Along with large telescopes on the ground on Earth, astronomers also use telescopes positioned out in space. By placing these instruments in space, astronomers are able to get around many of the problems faced by earthbound telescopes. Plus, since there is no night or day in space, astronomers can use them at any time!

A BLURRED EFFECT

From the ground, the Earth's atmosphere causes problems when looking out into space, since it is always moving around, which slightly blurs the light passing through it. When looking through a telescope, this blurring makes it difficult to see any clearly defined objects. The Earth's atmosphere also blocks some parts of the electromagnetic spectrum, including ultraviolet or X-rays. Many objects in the universe put out these rays, and they can only be studied by putting specially built telescopes into space. Telescopes in space are also not affected by the glare of city lights or the effects of weather, such as clouds and rain.

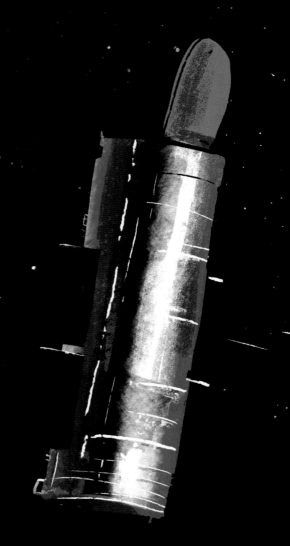

HUBBLE SPACE TELESCOPE

The Hubble Space Telescope was the first large optical telescope to be placed into space. Launched on April 24, 1990, onboard the space shuttle *Discovery*, it went into orbit at a height of 329 miles (530 km) above Earth. Traveling at a speed of 16,963 mph (27,300 kph), the telescope completed one lap around Earth in just 95 minutes.

The Hubble Telescope's main mirror is 7.8 ft (2.4 m) in diameter and can detect infrared and ultraviolet light. Using the space shuttle missions, astronauts visited the telescope five times between 1993 and 2009 to service it and replace parts. The telescope has been in operation for over 30 years and has been amazingly successful. More than 1.5 million observations of the universe have been made with Hubble, and it has beamed back countless beautiful images of planets, stars, and galaxies.

CHANDRA X-RAY TELESCOPE

On July 23, 1999, NASA launched a special telescope into space that could detect X-rays coming from very hot objects in the universe. Called the Chandra X-ray Observatory, it is 43 ft (13 m) long and orbits 86,370 miles (139,000 km) above Earth. Astronomers use the Chandra telescope to study X-rays from exploding stars, groups of galaxies, and matter that's spiraling around black holes.

SPITZER SPACE TELESCOPE

In 2003, NASA launched another amazing space telescope built to detect infrared light. Named the Spitzer Space Telescope, the mission lasted until 2020. It sent back amazing views of star-making regions in space and the centers of galaxies. The Spitzer telescope also helped astronomers learn more about how planets are made.

JAMES WEBB SPACE TELESCOPE

On December 25, 2021, the largest and most powerful space telescope ever built was launched. The James Webb Space Telescope (JWST) took many years to plan and build, and brought together scientists and engineers from NASA, the European Space Agency (ESA), and the Canadian Space Agency. This powerful infrared telescope can see very far into the universe, as well as deep into very dusty clouds called nebulae. Astronomers use the Webb telescope to study how planets, stars, and galaxies were made.

WORKING IN DEEP SPACE

After launch, it took 30 days for the Webb telescope to travel the 93 million miles (1.5 million km) to reach its permanent home in space. Once in place, scientists sent signals from Earth to open up its huge 21-ft- (6.5-m-) wide mirror. The Webb telescope mirror is actually made of 18 smaller mirrors that had to be perfectly lined up. The telescope gets its power from 20-ft- (6-m-) wide solar panels.

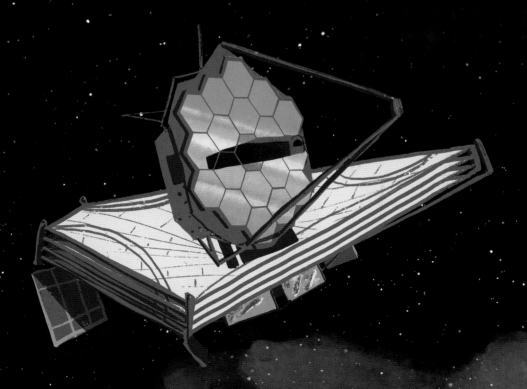

WEBB WONDERS

By the end of its first year of observation, the Webb telescope had already beamed back spectacular images of the universe! Its first hits included amazingly detailed images of the insides of huge pillars of gas and dust, where brand-new stars are forming. The infrared views show knots of gas that are starting to squeeze together under gravity and are slowly heating up to form new stars.

The Webb telescope has also taken the deepest image in infrared light we have ever seen, looking back 13 billion years to a time when galaxies were being made in a very young universe. The telescope has also given us the clearest views of Neptune's rings. Not since the *Voyager 2* spacecraft flew by Neptune in 1989 have we seen the gas planet's rings in such clear detail.

**Webb's view
of Neptune and its rings**

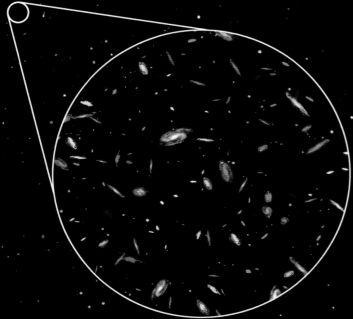

**Webb's view
of deep space**

THE SOLAR SYSTEM

The solar system is our neighborhood in space. It is an amazing collection of planets, dwarf planets, moons, comets, asteroids, dust, and gas that move around our local star, the Sun.

The solar system began to form about 4.6 billion years ago, when a giant cloud of gas and dust known as a nebula started to squeeze together by the force of gravity. More and more material was pulled into the center of the crushed nebula, where the gas became extremely hot. The Sun formed in the center, using up more than 99 percent of all the mass of the solar system. The planets were made in a thin platelike disk of swirling material that orbited around

Four rocky planets—Mercury, Venus, Earth, and Mars—were forged in the inner part of the solar system. Much farther out, where it was cooler and icy, the giant gas planets Jupiter, Saturn, Uranus, and Neptune were assembled. Along with dwarf planets such as Pluto, the outermost regions of the solar system became home to swarms of frozen comets.

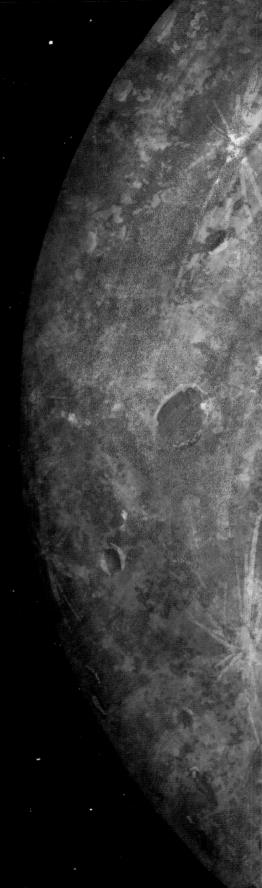

MERCURY

Mercury is the closest planet to the Sun. It is also the tiniest planet, with a radius of **1,516** miles (2,440 km), making it only slightly larger than Earth's Moon. Mercury has the most oval orbit of all the planets. Days on Mercury are very long because it spins on its axis so slowly—one day on Mercury lasts for **59** Earth days!

HOT AND COLD

The side of Mercury facing the Sun can reach scorching temperatures of 806 degrees Fahrenheit [°F] (430 degrees Celsius [°C]), which is hot enough to melt lead! However, because Mercury is too small to have a proper atmosphere, this heat does not reach the dark side of the planet that faces away from the Sun. There, the temperature can drop down to a truly freezing -274 °F (-170 °C)!

THERE'S ICE THERE!

It may be close to the Sun, but Mercury is very cold near its north and south poles. Sunlight never reaches the bottom of some craters! Scientists have discovered that water in the form of ice is present in parts of craters that are permanently in shadow.

MOONLIKE

The surface of Mercury looks similar to that of Earth's Moon. The planet had active volcanoes for the first billion years after it formed, but it has been quiet ever since. Mercury's largest crater is named Caloris Basin. It is 932 miles (1,500 km) in diameter and was formed when a rocky object about 93 miles (150 km) across smashed into Mercury more than 3 billion years ago.

METAL BALL

Mercury has a metallic inner core similar to that of Earth. One big difference is that Mercury's metal core fills nearly 85 percent of the total volume of the planet. Using new data sent back by spacecraft, scientists believe that Mercury not only has a liquid core, but also a solid inner core almost the same size as Earth's.

VENUS

Venus is the second planet from the Sun and one of the four rocky (or terrestrial) planets. It is the hottest planet in the solar system, with a crushing atmosphere and volcanism. Shining brighter than any other planet in the night sky, Venus is named after the Roman goddess of love and beauty.

Earth   **Venus**

SISTER PLANETS

Venus is the Earth's closest planetary neighbor. It's sometimes called Earth's sister because the two planets have a similar size and mass—Venus has a diameter of 7,518 miles (12,100 km) compared to Earth's diameter of 7,922 miles (12,750 km). The gravity on Venus is only one-tenth weaker than on Earth. Venus, however, does not have a moon.

CLIMATE CRISIS!

When it comes to climate, weather, and atmosphere, Venus and Earth are very different worlds. Venus has a thick, harsh atmosphere filled with carbon dioxide. It is always totally covered with yellow clouds mostly made of sulphuric acid. Droplets of sulphuric acid rain down through the atmosphere.

Temperatures on the surface of Venus can reach 887 °F (475 °C). The thick atmosphere forms a blanket around the planet that acts like a greenhouse to trap in heat from the Sun. At the surface, the pressure from the very thick atmosphere is a crushing 93 times greater than the pressure we feel on Earth.

EXPLORING THE SURFACE

Viewed from Earth, the clouds around Venus block any views of its surface. We got our first and only direct glimpses of Venus' surface when the Soviet Union (now Russia) sent five spacecraft named *Venera* to land there between October 1975 and March 1982. Each *Venera* landing craft only lasted a few hours because of the scorching temperature and extremely high pressure. Many years later, astronomers were able to map out most of the planet's surface using space missions such as *Magellan*, which used radar to see through the planet's thick clouds.

HOT, DRY PLAINS

Most of Venus' surface is made of rolling plains that have been covered by ancient lava flows. Scientists believe volcanoes have been erupting there within the past 300 million years, and a few still might be active today. Venus has several mountains. The highest, called Maxwell Montes, rises 6.8 miles (11 km) above the surface—that is over a mile higher than Earth's highest mountain, Mount Everest.

There are few craters on Venus—the planet's thick atmosphere burns up small objects from space before they are able to crash into the surface. There are around a thousand fairly large known craters, one of the largest being Mead Crater. It is about 168 miles (270 km) in diameter, with a 0.62 mile (1 km) drop from the rim of the crater to its floor.

PLANET EARTH

Our home planet, Earth, is a very special and beautiful world. It is the only place in the universe where we know for sure life exists. The Earth is the only planet in the solar system with surface oceans of liquid water and an atmosphere with plenty of oxygen.

CALENDAR DAYS

Earth is the third rocky planet from the Sun and the fifth largest in the solar system. It takes 365 and a quarter days to orbit the Sun once. We add an extra day every four years to allow for the extra quarter day in our calendars. Our planet spins on its axis every 24 hours, giving us day and night as it turns.

CHANGING SURFACE

The surface of the Earth has mountains, valleys, and volcanoes. Almost 70 percent of the planet's surface is covered by liquid water. Most of the water is contained in vast oceans, but it's also in rivers, lakes, ice caps, and glaciers.

Earth's surface is active and ever-changing. The upper crust layer is made of several plates that fit tightly together and move slowly. The plates can collide, split apart, or slide against each other. This movement gives us earthquakes, explosive volcanoes, and huge lava flows.

AIR WE CAN BREATHE

Earth's atmosphere is about 78 percent nitrogen, 21 percent oxygen, and 1 percent other gases such as carbon dioxide. The atmosphere protects us from harmful X-rays and ultraviolet light from the Sun, while also keeping Earth's temperature comfortable for life. Rocky bodies heading toward Earth from space are burned up in the atmosphere before they can reach us.

MANY LAYERS

The Earth formed about 4.5 billion years ago out of the same giant cloud of gas and dust that made the Sun and the rest of the solar system. Over millions and billions of years, as the Earth slowly cooled down, its interior settled into four distinct layers.

At the planet's center is an inner core, which is a solid ball of iron and nickel of about a 758-mile- (1,220-km-) radius. The temperature in the inner core is 10,832 °F (6,000 °C), which is about the same as the surface of the Sun. Above the inner core is a layer called the outer core, which is mainly liquid iron and nickel. The core is surrounded by a mantle, which is a 1,802-mile- (2,900-km-) thick layer of molten rock. The uppermost rocky layer of Earth is the crust, where the thickness can be between 3 miles (5 km) and 50 miles (80 km).

A BIG MAGNET

As the Earth spins, its core of metals forms a magnetic field that stretches above and around the planet. The magnetic field shields us from high-energy particles from the Sun. The particles get locked into the magnetic field and get funneled toward the Earth's north and south poles. As they glide down, the particles smash with gases in our atmosphere to make shimmering, colorful lights called auroras. These are also known as the northern and southern lights.

MARS

Mars, often referred to as the Red Planet, is the fourth and most distant rocky planet from the Sun. It is a dusty desert world, with two little moons and a thin atmosphere made mostly of carbon dioxide. Mars takes **687** Earth days to orbit once around the Sun, which means that its year is almost twice as long as ours. Mars is almost two times smaller than Earth, with a diameter of around **4,219** miles (6,790 km). During the year, as the seasons change, the temperature on the surface of Mars can range between **−220** °F (−140 °C) and **86** °F (30 °C.)

THE RED PLANET

Mars was named by the Romans after their fearsome god of war, but in truth, they were somewhat inspired by the ancient Greeks, who called it Ares after their own war god. Chinese astronomers knew the planet as the "fire star," whilst in ancient Egypt, the planet was called "Her desher," meaning "the red one." The surface of Mars is covered in soil that contains a lot of iron oxide. It is the same mixture of iron and oxygen that creates the reddish-brown rust you sometimes see forming on metal.

RECORD BREAKER

Mars is home to the tallest known extinct volcano, Olympus Mons. It is 16 miles (25 km) high and 373 miles (600 km) diameter at its base—it is three times the height of the tallest mountain on Earth, Mount Everest. The Red Planet also experiences the largest, most violent dust storms of any planet. During some seasons, the storms are so huge that the entire planet can be covered. Finally, there is a canyon on Mars named Valles Marineris, which is twenty times wider and five times deeper than the Grand Canyon in the United States.

ICE CAPS

Like Earth, Mars has ice caps at its north and south poles. Water in the poles is frozen into thin layers that gradually build up. Mixed with this water is dust picked up by the wind on Mars. During the Martian winter, it gets so cold at the poles that carbon dioxide freezes from the atmosphere and forms more layers of "dry ice."

One of the most exciting discoveries made on Mars is that liquid water flowed on its surface some 3 to 4 billion years ago. We can see the evidence of this today in the channels, valleys, and gullies carved by erosion from the moving water. Though all this water has long since evaporated, some liquid water remains beneath its surface. Many spacecraft have been sent to explore the surface of Mars and search for signs that bacterial life may have once existed there.

Named after the king of the ancient Roman gods, Jupiter is a spectacular planet. It is the third-brightest object in the night sky after Venus and the Moon, and is a great target to study with binoculars or a small telescope. With an average distance of 483 million miles (777 million km) from the Sun, it is the fifth planet from the star. Jupiter lies five times farther away from the Sun than Earth, between the orbits of Mars and Saturn.

MASSIVE AND HUGE!

Jupiter is the most massive and the largest planet in the solar system. Its diameter is 11 times that of Earth and its mass is two and a half times greater than all the other planets in the solar system combined! Mass affects gravity, so Jupiter also has very strong gravity. The gravitational pull of this giant gas planet affects every other planet in the solar system—it tears up asteroids and keeps many moons held around the planet.

RINGS

Everyone has heard of Saturn's rings, but did you know that Jupiter has rings too? There are four sets of rings around the giant planet, the main one being just 4,038 miles (6,500 km) wide. These rings are made of small, very dark particles that are very difficult to see.

STRANGE INTERIOR

Because Jupiter is a giant gas planet, you cannot simply land on it as you would on a terrestrial planet. Its interior is mostly made of hydrogen and helium, and as you go deeper into the planet, the pressure and temperature really start to rise. Under huge pressures, the hydrogen begins to act like a liquid and then a metal. Astronomers believe that Jupiter has a central core that's a soup of superhot rocky material

PATTERNS AND SPOTS

Jupiter's appearance is truly amazing, thanks to its colorful cloud bands and spots. The top of Jupiter's atmosphere is made up of three main cloud layers that have a combined thickness of 43 miles (70 km). The layers are made of ammonia crystals, ammonia ice, and water ice. The planet spins very fast, with a day on Jupiter lasting slightly less than 10 hours. The spin helps the cloud layers form a pattern of bands around the planet. There are also many spotlike or oval features—these are cyclones and storms. The most famous storm system on Jupiter is called the Great Red Spot. This storm extends 310 miles (500 km) deep in the atmosphere and is so huge that you could fit Planet Earth across it!

Earth (shown for scale)

Europa **Callisto**

Io **Ganymede**

MOONS GALORE

Jupiter has 95 known moons. Though about 50 of them are only 6 miles (10 km) or so wide, it also has some of the largest moons in the solar system. Biggest among these are Io, Europa, Ganymede, and Callisto. They were first discovered by the astronomer Galileo Galilei in 1610 using an early version of a telescope.

SATURN

Saturn is the second-largest planet in the solar system, with a diameter around nine times bigger than Earth's. This giant planet is mostly made of hydrogen and helium gas. The sixth planet from the Sun, Saturn is found 866 million miles (1.4 billion km) from the star, which means it is almost 10 times farther from Earth than we are from the Sun. Still, out of the five planets beyond Earth that we can see in the night sky just using our eyes, Saturn is the most distant. The planet has at least 100 moons of all shapes and sizes. The largest, Titan, is bigger than Mercury.

RINGS GALORE

Viewed through binoculars or even a small telescope, Saturn looks stunning. It has 10 continuous main rings that extend from 41,000 miles (66,000 km) to 87,000 miles (140,000 km) from the center of the planet. The rings are mostly made of water ice, dust, and rocks. They are very flat compared to the enormous round shape of Saturn overall, with each ring being between 33 ft (10 m) and 3,273 ft (1,000 m) thick.

ATMOSPHERE

From Earth, Saturn has a banded, yellow appearance.
It gets its golden-yellow color from ammonia crystals
in the upper layers of its atmosphere. There is a lot of
activity going on in these layers. Winds can rage at a
blistering speed of 1,118 mph (1,800 kph) and single
storms can last for more than a year. Lightning strikes
on Saturn can be a thousand times more powerful
than those we see on Earth. Saturn's north pole has
an incredible hexagon-shaped storm, where each
side of the hexagon is 8,575 miles (13,800 km) long.
That's wider than the diameter of the Earth!

GOING DEEPER

Being a gas giant, Saturn does not have a rocky
surface beneath its clouds and upper atmosphere.
Farther inward, as the pressure gets higher, the
hydrogen starts to act like a liquid and then becomes
metallic. The temperature toward the center can be
as high as 19,292 °F (10,700 °C), which is hotter than
the surface of the Sun! At Saturn's center is a dense
core of metals, such as iron and nickel.

URANUS

Uranus is an icy giant and the third-largest planet in the solar system. Named after the Greek god of the heavens, Ouranos, it is the only planet not named for a Roman god. Uranus orbits the Sun at a distance of around 1.8 billion miles (3 billion km) or 20 times the distance from Earth to the Sun. NASA's *Voyager 2* is the only spacecraft to have visited Uranus. In 1986, it flew past the gas planet and made many new discoveries about its atmosphere, rings, and moons.

DIAMOND RAIN

The atmosphere of Uranus is mostly made up of hydrogen and helium. It also contains methane, which gives the planet its beautiful blue-green color. This atmosphere is topped by thick icy clouds.

As you go deeper into the atmosphere, the methane gas breaks apart, and the carbon atoms from the methane are squeezed together so tightly that they create diamonds. The diamonds rain thousands of miles (km) into the inner layers of Uranus, like very special hailstones!

DARK RINGS

Uranus has a set of 13 dark rings made of small particles and water. They are mostly very narrow and just a few miles (km) wide. Astronomers think that the rings formed when moons collided and were ripped apart by gravity. The leftovers from these smashups went into orbit around Uranus, forming the rings.

A ROLLING BARREL

Most planets in the solar system turn on their axis like a spinning top. Uranus, however, has toppled over and is rolling like a barrel in its orbit around the Sun. Scientists believe that a large body about the size of Earth crashed into Uranus billions of years ago and knocked it over.

LITERARY MOONS

Uranus has 28 known moons, and they are all named after characters from literature by William Shakespeare and Alexander Pope. Its five large moons are named Miranda, Ariel, Umbriel, Oberon, and Titania. Titania is the biggest of the moons, with a diameter of 982 miles (1,580 km).

   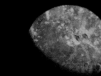

Miranda   **Ariel**   **Umbriel**   **Oberon**   **Titania**

SEASONS

The axis or imaginary line that connects the north and south poles of Neptune is similar to that on Earth and Mars. This means that Neptune also has seasons, which can lead to changes in its temperature and climate. A big difference, however, is that summer, winter, fall, and spring each last for more than 40 years on Neptune!

NEPTUNE

Neptune is the smallest of the gas giant planets and also the farthest away. It's a very strange and mysterious world, orbiting the Sun 30 times farther out in the solar system than Earth does. At this great distance, it takes Neptune about 165 Earth years to complete a single orbit around the Sun. It is also four times larger than Earth. Our only close-up view of the planet was taken in August 1989, when NASA's *Voyager 2* spacecraft flew past it.

STORMY WORLD

Much like Uranus, Neptune's atmosphere is mostly made of hydrogen and helium gas. Smaller amounts of methane also give Neptune its blue color, which is deeper and darker than Uranus's. There are violent storms and fierce winds blowing on Neptune. In 1989, the *Voyager 2* spacecraft spotted a huge cyclone measuring 8,000 miles (12,875 km) wide, which is almost the diameter of Earth! Neptune has the strongest winds of any planet in the solar system, with winds reaching speeds of over 1,100 mph (1,770 kph)—one and a half times the speed of sound.

Much deeper down in its atmosphere, Neptune may have an ocean of superhot water and other melted ices. Scientists believe that it has a solid core that is about the size of Earth, and a magnetic field that is 27 times more powerful than that of Earth.

MOONS AND RINGS

Neptune has 16 known moons, many of which have very odd shapes and orbits. With a diameter of 1,678 miles (2,700 km), Triton is the largest of Neptune's moons—it is also one of the coldest in the solar system. The temperature on the surface of Triton is a freezing −391 °F (−235 °C)! On occasions, the moon spews out icy material that rises more than 5 miles (8 km) above the surface.

Neptune has at least five main rings, each made of dust and small rocks. They are very dark and hard to see. The rings are likely to have formed from leftover material after some of the planet's original moons crashed into each other.

COMETS

The word *comet* comes from the Greek *kometes*, meaning "long-haired." It is named for its dramatic appearance, which is like a bright star with a tail of hair flowing behind it. Centuries ago, the sight of a comet in the night sky inspired great fear, since it was believed to be a warning of disaster. Comets also feature in the stories and art of many different cultures.

ANCIENT LEFTOVERS

Today, we know that comets are objects made up of leftover matter from the formation of the Sun and planets some 4.6 billion years ago. The study of comets is very important, because it helps us to learn how our solar system was assembled.

DIRTY SNOWBALLS

Comets are large balls of rock, ice, dust, and gases. The solid center of a comet is called a nucleus—think of it as a large, dirty snowball, where the icy matter is loosely held together. The nucleus can range in size from 300 ft (90 m) across to several miles (kilometers).

HOMES OF COMETS

Our solar system is surrounded by a vast spherical shell known as the Oort cloud. It stretches between 2,000 and 5,000 times the distance between the Earth and the Sun. This extremely cold cloud in the most remote part of our solar system is home to billions or trillions of comets. Closer in, beyond the orbit of Neptune, there is another home of comets in a doughnut-shaped region known as the Kuiper Belt.

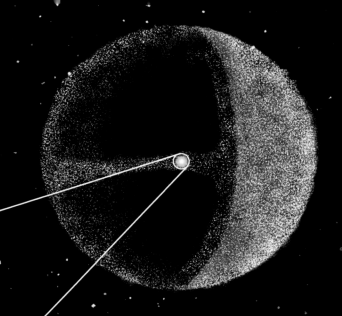

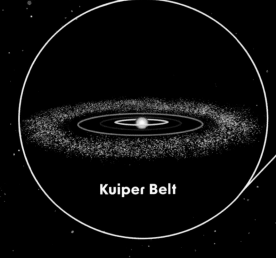

Kuiper Belt

GROWING A TAIL

Sometimes, comets in the Oort cloud or Kuiper Belt get knocked out and fall toward the inner solar system. The dislodged comets travel in long, egg-shaped orbits, bringing them much closer to the Sun. Heat from the Sun turns their frozen ice into a huge halo of dust and gas called a coma.

As the comet gets closer to the Sun, it grows a tail. Sunlight and superfast particles from the Sun (known as the solar wind) pushes dust and gas off the coma, creating a tail. And this is why a comet's tail always points away from the Sun—a little bit like streamers attached to a desk fan. The tail can stretch over 621,000 miles (1,000,000 km), resulting in a beautiful show in our night sky.

FAMOUS COMETS

One of the most famous comets, Comet Halley, last appeared in our skies in 1986. It is named after English astronomer Edmund Halley, who first worked out its orbit in the seventeenth century. Comet Halley will next return in 2061.

A comet named Shoemaker-Levy 9 crashed into Jupiter in 1994, and for a few weeks, the scars of the cosmic smash could be seen in the upper cloud layers of the giant planet. Spacecraft have also visited comets (*see pp. 82–83*). In 2006, a NASA spacecraft named *Stardust* brought samples of dust from Comet Wild 2 back to Earth.

Most comets pass around the Sun and head back to the outer solar system on long, looping orbits, once again becoming cold, dark objects. However, occasionally a few comets stray too close to the Sun and crash into it!

ASTEROIDS, METEOROIDS, AND METEORS

Some of the material floating around in the solar system is in the form of small rocky objects known as asteroids and meteoroids. These are mostly leftovers from the dawn of the solar system, when the planets and moons formed around **4.5** billion years ago. If the object is larger than **3.2** ft (1 m), then it is an asteroid. Smaller than that, it is a meteoroid, which are frequently only millimeters (inches) in size.

A GREAT BELT

Most of the asteroids in the solar system are found in a region between Mars and Jupiter known as the asteroid belt. It contains millions of pieces of rock and metal. The largest asteroids found here, such as Vesta, Pallas, and Hygiea, are more than 248 miles (400 km) long. All the objects scattered in the asteroid belt orbit the Sun. If you gathered up all the asteroids and meteroids in the asteroid belt, their combined mass would be less than that of Earth's Moon.

Asteroids can teach us how planets and moons formed. Over the past two decades, many spacecraft missions have been sent to fly close to asteroids. Some have even landed on them, while others have returned samples back to Earth for scientists to study in laboratories. It seems that most asteroids are like piles of rubble loosely held together by gravity, rather than solid chunks.

METEORITES ON EARTH

When a meteoroid is large enough to survive the trip through the Earth's atmosphere and hit the ground, the piece that lands is called a meteorite. The best places to find meteorites on Earth are in large sandy deserts or icy frozen plains, where the very dark meteorites stand out more clearly.

METEOR SHOWERS

Occasionally, tiny meteoroids enter the Earth's atmosphere, traveling at very high speeds and burning up in displays of fireballs in the sky. Also known as "shooting stars," these fiery displays are meteors. At certain times of the year, the frequency and number of meteors in the sky can be very high. These magical displays are called meteor showers, a famous example of which is the Perseids meteor shower, which peaks in August in the northern hemisphere every year.

DWARF PLANETS

One of the reasons the universe is so exciting is that there are so many varied and amazing objects in it. The same is true for our solar system. Along with a variety of planets, moons, comets, and asteroids, there are also beautiful little icy worlds called dwarf planets. Pluto is the most famous dwarf planet.

THE GOLDEN RULE

Dwarf planets are all small—Pluto is two times smaller than Mercury, the smallest planet in the solar system. Like planets, they mostly have similar round or near-round shapes. When comparing dwarf planets with "standard" planets, the biggest difference is that dwarf planets have not cleared the area of objects in their path around the Sun, unlike planets, which do not share their orbit with other bodies.

There are five confirmed dwarf planets in the solar system, but there could be many tens more waiting to be added to the list. Let's take a closer look at the five we know about.

MAKEMAKE

Taking 305 years to orbit the Sun, Makemake is 444 miles (715 km) in diameter. The Hubble Space Telescope discovered it has a tiny moon, just 50 miles (80 km) wide. We cannot see many surface details of this dwarf planet, but it is thought to be a reddish-brown color.

HAUMEA

The fifth confirmed dwarf planet is called Haumea. It is spinning very fast, turning once in less than four hours. This fast spin has squashed Haumea into an egg-like shape. It has two moons and may even have a ring.

PLUTO

When Pluto was first discovered in 1930, it was named the ninth planet of the solar system. It was renamed as a dwarf planet in 2006, when astronomers brought in new rules for defining a planet. Pluto has five moons, the largest of which is Charon. In July 2015, NASA's *New Horizon* spacecraft sent back amazing pictures of icy plains and mountains on Pluto, made of nitrogen ice and water ice.

Earth's Moon (shown for scale)

ERIS

The dwarf planet Eris is farther away than Neptune and takes 557 years to complete one lap around the Sun. It is only slightly smaller than Pluto. Astronomers think that Eris has lots of methane ice and water ice.

CERES

Ceres is our closest known dwarf planet. Located in the asteroid belt between Mars and Jupiter, it is 588 miles (946 km) across, which is about a third of the size of Earth's Moon. Ceres may have an ocean of liquid water beneath its icy surface.

57

WORLDS AROUND OTHER STARS

When our Sun formed out of a giant cloud of gas and dust, some of the leftover matter created planets and the rest of the objects in the solar system. When other stars were made, they too would have had spare material leftover to make planets. A planet that is in orbit around a star that is not our Sun is known as an exoplanet.

THE EXOPLANET ZOO

Astronomers have so far discovered about 5,600 exoplanets in the Milky Way. Since there are 200 billion stars in our galaxy, astronomers believe there may be millions or billions of exoplanets out there!

The exoplanets are much too small and faint for us to takes images of them using telescopes. Instead, they are detected by how they change the light of their parent star, or how the gravity of the exoplanets tugs on their star.

Out of the exoplanets discovered so far, some are massive gas giants similar to Jupiter, while others are rocky and maybe even Earth-like in size. There are also molten hot planets and ocean worlds that may contain huge amounts of water. Some exoplanets are nothing like any planet in our solar system.

Trappist-1

Trappist-1e

GOLDILOCKS PLANETS

As far as we are aware, Earth is the only planet that has life. As water is a very important ingredient for life on our planet, astronomers are looking for exoplanets that may also have liquid water on their surfaces. For an exoplanet to have oceans or large lakes of water, it must be at just the right temperature and distance from its star. These exoplanets are called Goldilocks planets, since (just like Goldilock's porridge in the fairy tale) they are not too hot or too cold. They are just right for liquid water to be present on the surface.

TRAPPIST SYSTEM

There is an exciting group of planets just beyond our solar system, about 40 light-years away. That's still too far for us to travel to, but it's close enough that we can learn a lot about it using powerful telescopes. This system is called TRAPPIST, and it is made up of seven exoplanets. They all orbit very tightly around a small and cool red dwarf star named TRAPPIST-1.

The planets in TRAPPIST orbit so closely to their star that if they were placed in our solar system, all seven would fit within the distance between the Sun and Mercury! Their orbits are so small that the innermost exoplanet takes just 36 hours to complete an orbit around its star.

TRAPPIST-1E

The planet known as TRAPPIST-1e has almost the same size, mass, and gravity as Earth. It is a rocky planet with a similar temperature to our planet. TRAPPIST-1e is one of the most Earth-like planets we know of so far, and astronomers believe it may be a Goldilocks planet, with liquid water on its surface. The powerful James Webb Space Telescope (*see pp. 32–33*) will be used to help us learn more about the TRAPPIST planet system.

MOONS ACROSS THE SOLAR SYSTEM

A moon is a natural satellite that makes an orbit around a planet, a dwarf planet, or a minor object such as an asteroid. Earth's one Moon is a familiar sight in our sky—but did you know there are more than 300 known moons in our solar system?

Out of all the planets, Jupiter and Saturn have the most moons—a total of almost 200 between them. Uranus and Neptune have more than 40 moons in total, Pluto has five, while Mars has just two tiny moons. Other dwarf planets and many asteroids also have tiny moons.

The moons of the solar system come in a variety of shapes, sizes, and types. They have some amazing landscapes, interiors, and surfaces, and a few have atmospheres and oceans of liquid water hidden beneath their thick, icy surfaces.

The moons orbiting planets mostly formed from the disks of gas and dust that swirled around newborn planets in the early solar system. Some moons were captured and pulled into orbits by the strong gravity of the largest planets.

EARTH'S MOON

The Moon is Earth's constant companion in space as it orbits the Sun. With a diameter of **2,160** miles (3,476 km), it is almost a quarter the size of the Earth and is the fifth-largest moon in the solar system. The Moon orbits our planet at a distance of **238,855** miles (384,400 km). If the Earth was the size of a basketball, the Moon would be the size of a tennis ball, sitting 24.2 ft (7.4 m) away.

SURFACE FEATURES

Even though the Moon is a few hundred thousand miles from Earth, some of its surface features can be seen just using our eyes. The dark patches you can see are called mare (pronounced "mar-ray," meaning "seas" in Latin). However, the mare are not seas of water—billions of years ago, they were seas of molten lava. The lava cooled and turned into solid rock a long time ago. Today, these areas appear as dark, smooth patches. The brighter regions of the Moon's surface are called highlands. They are the older and rougher parts of the surface.

Today, the surface of the Moon is covered in many thousands of craters. These are bowl-shaped dents made when rocky objects such as comets, asteroids, and meteoroids crashed there. Since the Moon has no atmosphere, winds, or rain, these ancient craters have not been eroded or washed away. A crater at the Moon's south pole named Aitken Basin covers almost a quarter of the area of the Moon, and it is deep enough to fit Earth's tallest mountain, Everest, inside it! Some of the craters, which stay cold and shadowed from sunlight, have water ice mixed in with the soil.

SAME SIDE

The Moon spins on its axis at the same rate that it revolves around the Earth. This means that the same side of the Moon faces the Earth at all times. Standing on Earth, we can never see the far side of the Moon.

ORIGIN

Scientists believe that the Moon formed about 4.5 billion years ago when a Mars-sized rock slammed into the Earth. The great force of the crash sent material from Earth's upper layers flying into space. Helped by the force of gravity, some of this debris stuck together, forming the Moon.

STRANGE LITTLE MOONS

There are some weird and wonderful moons in the solar system.
Not only do they come in a variety of shapes and sizes, their surfaces
can be quite unlike anything we could ever imagine on Earth.

CHARON

With a diameter of 752 miles (1,210 km), Charon is
the largest of the dwarf planet Pluto's five moons—it
is almost half the size of the dwarf planet itself.
Charon is so cold that any gas arriving there
immediately freezes on its surface. A single
mountain stands on Charon, as well as
a magnificent canyon that stretches
994 miles (1,600 km) around
its surface.

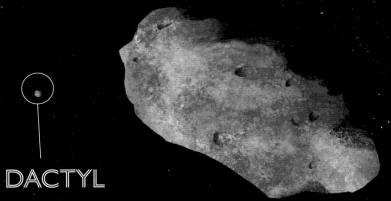

DACTYL

Dactyl is the first moon of an asteroid ever discovered. It orbits around an asteroid named Ida, which lies between Mars and Jupiter, and is just 0.93 miles (1.5 km) across. Astronomers think Dactyl is a lump of rock leftover from crashes between colliding asteroids.

PAN

Another odd-looking moon of the solar system is Pan. The innermost moon of Saturn, Pan is shaped like a ravioli! The icy moon is 19 miles (31 km) wide and orbits Saturn in a gap between the planet's rings.

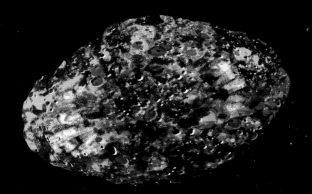

HYPERION

One of Saturn's strangest moons is named Hyperion—it looks like a potato-shaped sponge! Hyperion is about 255 miles (410 km) long and 161 miles (259 km) wide. It tumbles wildly as it orbits at great distances from Saturn. The surface of this strange moon has lots of very deep holes made by rocky objects, such as asteroids that crashed onto its surface many millions of years ago. These impacts created deep craters that gives Hyperion its strange spongelike appearance.

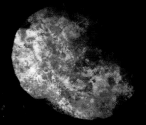

NEREID

Nereid is one of the most distant moons of Neptune. It is about 211 miles (340 km) in diameter and is so far out that it takes 360 Earth days to complete one orbit around the giant planet. And it has a very odd orbit, taking a long, skinny oval path. It is likely that Nereid is an asteroid that has been trapped by the gravity of Neptune.

ICY VOLCANOES

The active volcanoes we have on Earth spew out fiery rock, hot ash, and gases. However, another type of volcano exists in the solar system, and this one throws out icy water! Active ice volcanoes are found on some amazing moons in the outer parts of the solar system.

SNOW-WHITE ENCELADUS

With a diameter of 310 miles (499 km), Enceladus is Saturn's sixth-largest moon and one of the most remarkable objects in the solar system. Amazing discoveries about Enceladus were made when NASA's *Cassini* spacecraft explored Saturn, its rings, and moons between 2004 and 2017.

The surface of Enceladus is entirely covered in water ice, making it one of the whitest objects in the solar system. This frozen ocean world has a surface temperature of −328 °F (−200 °C). The *Cassini* spacecraft flew just 15.5 miles (25 km) above its surface and discovered huge plumes of water vapor being ejected from cracks in its surface—they are mostly seen around the moon's south pole. Most of this vapor escapes to form Saturn's second outermost ring, but some of the icy water drops back down to freshly cover Enceladus' freezing surface.

We are not sure what the interior of Enceladus is made of, but astronomers believe that there may be a huge amount of clear liquid beneath its icy crust, after noting that the temperature and pressure rises the deeper you go into the moon. Perhaps one day we will be able to tunnel through the thick icy crust and search for possible life-forms in its water oceans!

GUSHING TRITON

Powerful icy volcanoes are also erupting
on Neptune's largest moon, Triton. Once
more, ice and water play the role that rock,
lava, and magma do for volcanoes on Earth.
NASA's *Voyager 2* spacecraft took photos
of geysers spewing out 5-mile- (8-km-) tall
clouds of icy, dark particles. We don't know
much about how ice volcanoes form on
Triton, but they could be coming from an
ocean hidden beneath its rugged surface,
93 miles (150 km) deep and made
of water, ammonia, methane, and salts.

MOONS WITH OCEANS

One of the most exciting wonders of the solar system are moons that have enormous oceans hidden beneath their surfaces. Since life on Earth may have begun in our oceans, it is amazing to think that forms of life may also be present deep in these water-loaded moons!

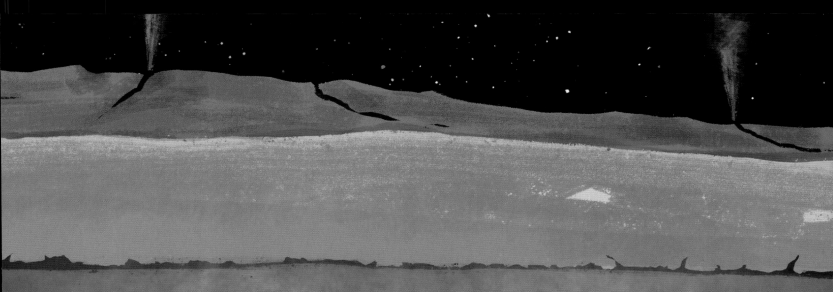

EXPLORING EUROPA

Jupiter's fourth largest moon, Europa, was discovered by Galileo Galilei in 1610. With a diameter of 1,926 miles (3,100 km), it is almost the same size as Earth's Moon. Many spacecraft have been flown past Europa to gather more information about its surface and the possible layers in its interior. The *Galileo* spacecraft made 12 close passes by Europa in the late 1990s, and from the images and measurements it sent back, it seems that Europa has a surface ice shell between 9.3 miles (15 km) and 15.5 miles (25 km) thick. This shell floats on an ocean of liquid water up to 93 miles (150 km) deep. Astronomers think that there may be twice as much water in this ocean than in all of Earth's oceans combined!

The enormous gravity of Jupiter acts to constantly squash and release Europa—a little bit like squashing and releasing a rubber ball in your hand. This flexing of Europa creates heat below its surface, keeping the water in liquid form. Scientists believe there may even be volcanoes and hot vents on the rocky floor beneath Europa's oceans. These eruptions not only create more heat, but also chemicals and minerals that can mix with the water, making the idea that life may exist there an even more exciting possibility.

NASA is planning to launch a new mission called *Clipper* to explore Europa. Arriving there in the early 2030s, it will make at least 45 very close flights past the moon, perhaps even passing through plumes of water rising from cracks in its surface.

MYSTERIOUS GANYMEDE

Jupiter's largest moon, Ganymede, is larger than Mercury and almost a quarter the size of Earth's diameter. It is also believed to have a huge ocean beneath its surface. But what's really mysterious is that Ganymede is the only moon in the solar system that makes its own magnetic field. It even has faint auroras, seen in a very thin atmosphere of oxygen. There may be many layers of salty water oceans and ice shells in the interior of Ganymede.

On April 14, 2023, the European Space Agency (ESA) launched a new mission called JUICE, and by around 2035 it is expected to go into orbit around Ganymede, traveling just 310 miles (499 km) above its surface. The spacecraft will send images and readings back to Earth about the moon's surface, icy eruptions, and its strange magnetic field.

SATURN'S TITAN

Named after the powerful giants of ancient Greek mythology, Titan is the largest of Saturn's many moons and the second-largest moon in the solar system. Titan is a really special world—it is the only known moon with a thick atmosphere and liquid lakes on its surface.

ORANGE HAZE

Other than Earth, Titan is the only other body in the solar system that has an atmosphere made of a large amount of nitrogen—almost 95 percent of its atmosphere is nitrogen gas, with the remainder mostly methane. There are also tiny amounts of other molecules made up of hydrogen and carbon atoms, such as ethane and propane, and these give Titan its distinctive orange haze. Some of the methane drops down through the atmosphere as rain.

OILY LAKES

The surface temperature of Titan is -290 °F (-179 °C), which is the perfect temperature for methane to take on its liquid form. The *Cassini* spacecraft studied Titan and discovered many methane lakes on its surface. They look like lakes made of oil!

The largest lake on Titan is known as Kraken Mare. It is can be found near the north pole of the moon, and its surface covers an area almost the size of Japan. Kraken Mare is about 525 ft (160 m) deep, with shallow waves rippling across it. Some of the oily lakes of Titan have rivers running from them, streaming toward lower ground.

The lakes contain lots of carbon and hydrogen. These chemicals were the ingredients for making amino acids and proteins on Earth, which then led to life. Scientists think that the Titan of today is what Earth was like billions of years ago.

FLIGHT OF THE DRAGONFLY

NASA is planning an exciting new mission called *Dragonfly* to study Titan. They plan to send a type of helicopter that has eight rotor blades. By 2035, it could be flying like a drone over the lakes and rivers of Titan. The *Dragonfly* will also explore the moon's atmosphere and look for clues to prove that life may have once existed there.

SPACECRAFT ACROSS THE SOLAR SYSTEM

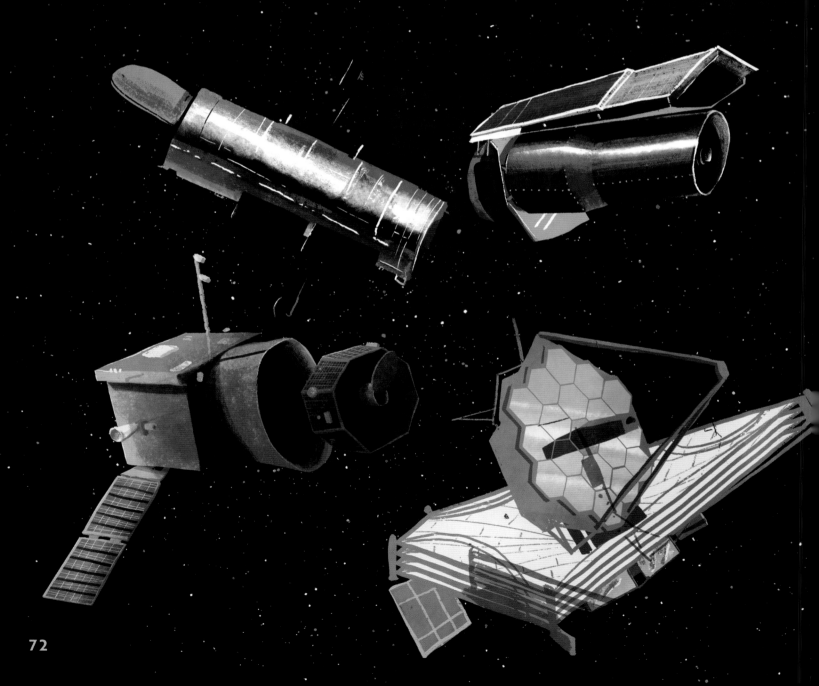

Over the last **60** years, our views and knowledge of the solar system have vastly improved, thanks to spacecraft missions we have sent across millions and billions of miles.

Using better technology, we have sent space probes to every planet, many moons, asteroids, and comets. We've sent landers and remote-controlled rovers to their surfaces and have even returned samples back to Earth. These missions have changed our view of the objects in the solar system from tiny specks in the night sky to beautiful, varied worlds. The information beamed back to Earth has allowed scientists to discover how the system formed and the way it works.

Also very exciting are the future missions being planned for the next few decades. Spacecraft will collect samples of soil and rocks from Mars, go into orbit around Uranus, and land on Saturn's icy moons. Meanwhile, humans may not only return to the surface of Earth's Moon, they could also soon make the first historic trip to Mars!

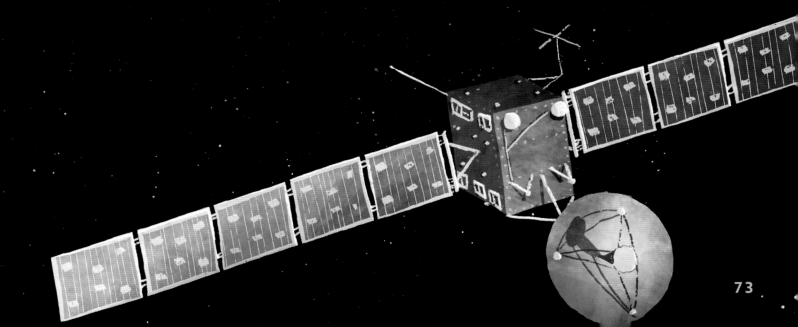

BEPICOLOMBO VISITS MERCURY

We know far less about Mercury than the other three rocky planets, Venus, Earth, and Mars. Mercury always appears very close to the glaring Sun in our skies, which makes it hard to view using telescopes. Flying spacecraft to Mercury is also tricky. The very strong pull from the gravity of the Sun makes it difficult to slow a spacecraft down and put it in orbit around the planet. And, once a spacecraft does get close to Mercury, it has to survive extreme heat. The spacecraft needs to be able to keep working in temperatures that can reach more than 392 °F (200 °C)!

A NEW LAUNCH

In 2018, the European and Japanese Space agencies jointly launched a new mission to explore Mercury. It is called *BepiColombo*, in honor of the Italian mathematician and engineer Guiseppi Colombo. The spacecraft is due to go into an orbit around Mercury in 2025. To get there, *BepiColombo* will make many flybys of Earth and Venus, using the gravity of both planets to pick up speed. It is also making six flybys of Mercury between 2021 and 2025 to get into orbit. Cooling pipes and special insulating blankets will be used to keep the instruments onboard from melting.

NEW FINDINGS TO COME

BepiColombo is packed with many scientific instruments to take new measurements of Mercury and beam them back to Earth. Some of them will be used to study the planet's magnetic field and find out what the atmosphere is made of. We will also get to see lots of amazing new images of Mercury's surface.

Astronomers hope to understand more about why Mercury has such a large core at its center and how the magnetic field is made. The mission will also teach us about the water ice that is present in the deep craters at the north and south poles. By studying Mercury, we can find out more about how the planets formed and what conditions were like when our solar system was very young.

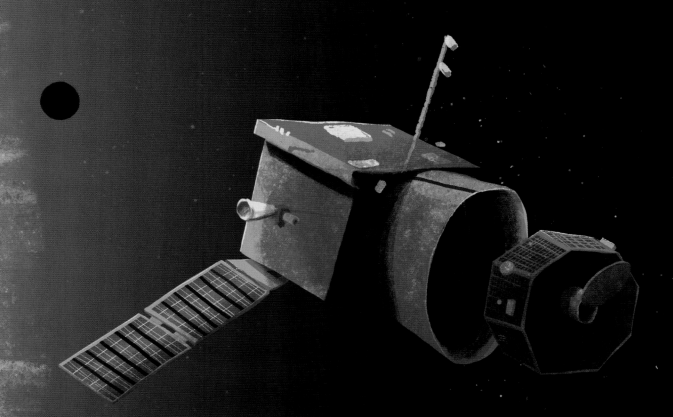

SAMPLING EARTH'S MOON

There is still much more to discover about how Earth's Moon formed into the beautiful object we now see in the night sky. Asteroids and comets slammed into the Moon over billions of years, and some of these may have carried water that is still present in the lunar soil. Discovering the resources available to us on the Moon, including water and minerals such as iron, is very important, since it could mean having to transport fewer materials on future missions in order to build bases there.

ROCK AND SOIL

While spacecraft placed in orbit around the Moon can send back lots of measurements, we can learn a great deal more by bringing back samples of rock and soil to Earth. Scientists can then study the Moon in their laboratories using very advanced technologies. A recent mission sent to the Moon to bring back samples was *Chang'e-5*, named after the Chinese moon goddess.

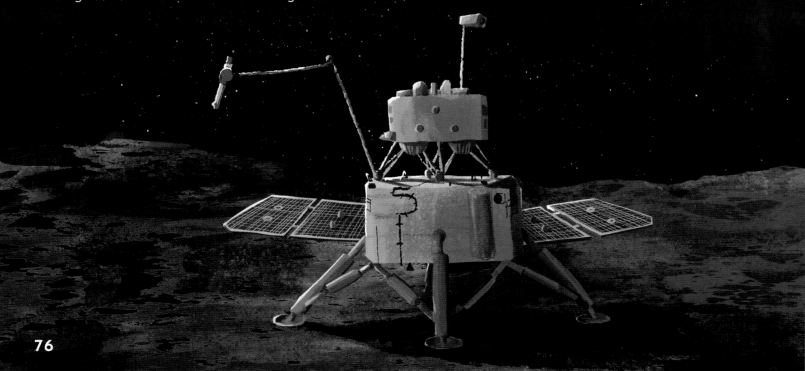

RETURNING MOON MATTER

Chang'e-5 was launched by the Chinese National Space Administration on November 23, 2020. Its mission was to bring the youngest samples of rock and soil from the Moon back to Earth. On December 1, 2020, the spacecraft landed on a dark gray region called the Ocean of Storms, where the material is only 1.2 billion years old. Rocks brought back by the Apollo astronauts in the 1970s were between 3 to 4 billion years old.

The *Chang'e-5* landing craft scooped up samples weighing 3.7 pounds [lb] (1.7 kilograms [kg]) and even drilled 6.5 ft (2 m) underground for some of the material. It then blasted off the surface and joined a service module that was in orbit around the Moon. A probe containing all the Moon samples was released from the service module to return to Earth. The probe went into orbit around Earth and released a capsule packed with Moon soil that landed safely in Mongolia, where it was picked up for scientists to study.

BEADS WITH WATER

Scientists have found that the soil brought back by the *Chang'e-5* spacecraft has lots of tiny glass beads in it. Each bead is about the width of a human hair, but amazingly, within the glass there was water! The beads and water are formed by tiny meteorites from space that slam into the Moon's surface, along with hydrogen streaming from the Sun.

Water is a very valuable resource to be able to use on the Moon, so this was an incredibly important discovery. Overall, there could be billions of tons of water that could be pulled out from the tiny beads, which could be used by astronauts on future missions to the Moon.

ROVERS ON MARS

Mars is a very exciting planet to explore and the most similar to Earth in the solar system. In the distant past, Mars once flowed with water, since it had a warmer climate and a much thicker atmosphere. Some living things may even have existed there. Today, Mars is a target for future human exploration. We need to understand more about the Red Planet so we can figure out if humans could live there in the future.

NIMBLE SPACE VEHICLES

One of the ways that scientists are learning about Mars is by using rovers placed on its surface. These rovers are remote-controlled vehicles that receive radio signals from Earth to guide them across the Martian surface. They can navigate the tricky terrain, collect samples, and conduct experiments. The results are then beamed back to scientists on Earth.

CURIOSITY

A car-sized rover named *Curiosity* touched down on Mars on August 6, 2012. Amazingly, it has been working on the planet's surface for more than 10 years. *Curiosity* has slowly traveled over 18.6 miles (30 km) and studied many different rock and soil samples. The rover made a special stop at a crater named Gale and discovered that there was once an ancient lake on the crater floor. It is a site where life may have been able to flourish in the past.

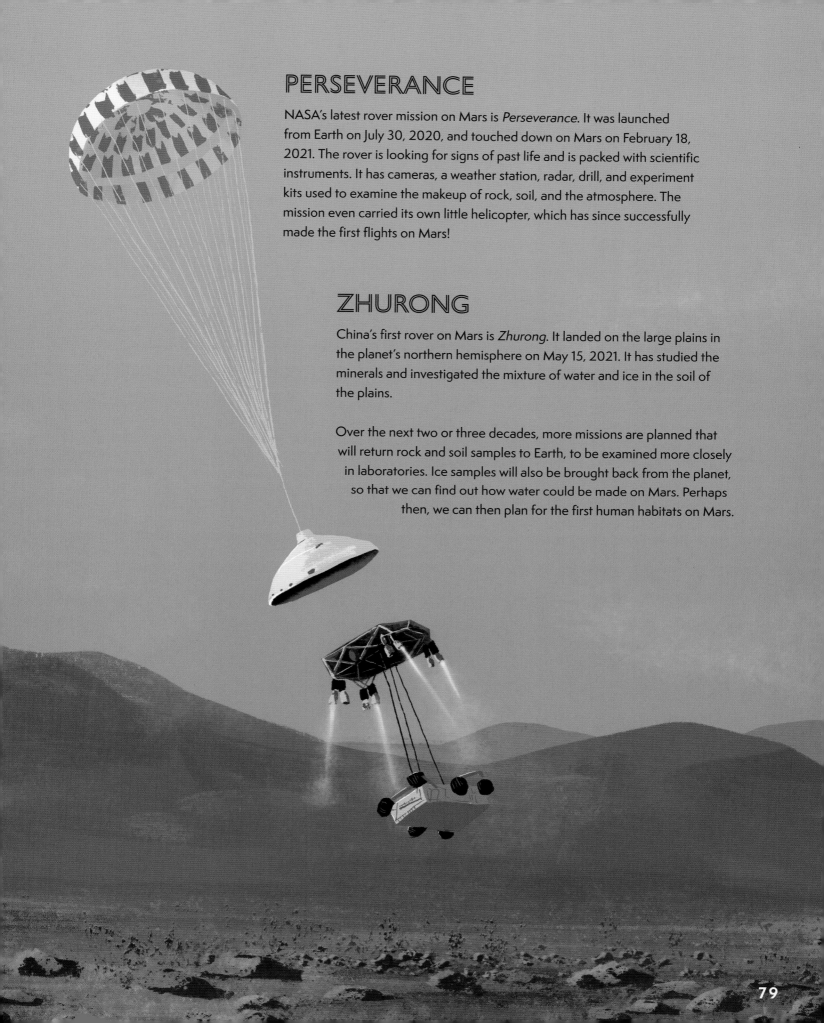

PERSEVERANCE

NASA's latest rover mission on Mars is *Perseverance*. It was launched from Earth on July 30, 2020, and touched down on Mars on February 18, 2021. The rover is looking for signs of past life and is packed with scientific instruments. It has cameras, a weather station, radar, drill, and experiment kits used to examine the makeup of rock, soil, and the atmosphere. The mission even carried its own little helicopter, which has since successfully made the first flights on Mars!

ZHURONG

China's first rover on Mars is *Zhurong*. It landed on the large plains in the planet's northern hemisphere on May 15, 2021. It has studied the minerals and investigated the mixture of water and ice in the soil of the plains.

Over the next two or three decades, more missions are planned that will return rock and soil samples to Earth, to be examined more closely in laboratories. Ice samples will also be brought back from the planet, so that we can find out how water could be made on Mars. Perhaps then, we can then plan for the first human habitats on Mars.

JUNO: UP CLOSE TO JUPITER

Our newest and most spectacular views of Jupiter have come from the spacecraft *Juno*, named after the wife of the mighty god Jupiter. Over the past few years, *Juno* has beamed back photographs and measurements to Earth, providing scientists with new information about the planet's atmosphere, storms, rings, and moons.

GETTING THERE

Juno was launched by NASA on August 5, 2011, blasting off from Cape Canaveral, USA, on a powerful Atlas V rocket. The spacecraft traveled almost 2 billion miles (3 billion km) in total before reaching Jupiter on July 4, 2016. On its way there, about a year after launch, *Juno* made a quick pass by Earth to get a boost from our planet's gravity—it acted like a slingshot, pushing *Juno* harder and faster toward Jupiter.

Juno gets its power from three enormous solar panels, each almost 29.5 ft (9 m) long and 8.8 ft (2.7 m) wide. The spacecraft has been in orbit around Jupiter since July 2016, making a pass around the giant planet every 53 days. The orbits can take *Juno* just 2,485 miles (4,000 km) above the atmosphere of Jupiter.

STORMS AND CYCLONES

Juno has taken amazing photos of the swirling clouds of water and ammonia around Jupiter. It has also witnessed many storms in the planet's atmosphere—there are huge cyclones around Jupiter's south pole, some wider than the United States! Measurements from *Juno* have taught scientists about Jupiter's inner layers, but very little is known about its core.

UP CLOSE

Juno has gotten very close to a faint ring around Jupiter and has also captured stunning views of the planet's giant moon Io, including detailed views of its active volcanoes. Swooping just 621 miles (1,000 km) above the surface of its moon Ganymede, *Juno* was able to photograph the mountains, craters, and valleys on its surface. The magnetic field of Jupiter has also been mapped out. *Juno* discovered a "great blue spot" on the giant planet, where the magnetic field is very strong.

JUNO'S FUTURE

Juno will never return to Earth. In September 2025, NASA will let it plunge into Jupiter's huge atmosphere.

THE ROSETTA MISSION

Rosetta was an exciting mission of "firsts." It was the first ever mission to follow a comet on its orbit around the Sun, and the first to successfully place a lander module on a comet's surface. The information gathered on this epic journey is helping us learn more about what comets are made of and how they are held together.

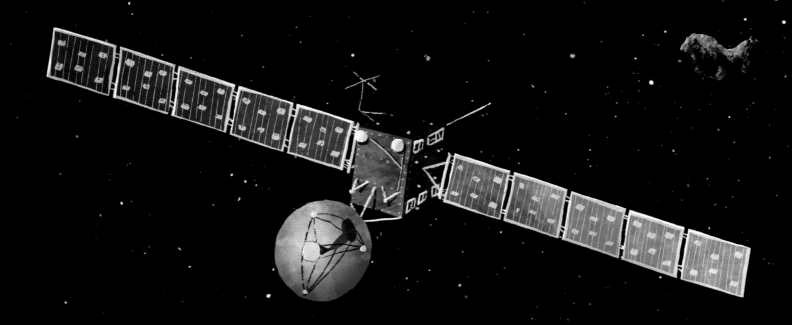

THE LONG JOURNEY

The *Rosetta* spacecraft had a very long and complicated journey to reach its target, a 2.4-mile-sized (4-km) comet named 67P/Churyumov-Gerasimenko, or 67P/C-G for short. The journey began on March 2, 2004, when *Rosetta* was launched by the European Space Agency (ESA) on a powerful Arianne 5 rocket.

Rosetta looped around the Sun three times and swung close by Earth and Mars to pick up more speed, assisted by the planets' gravity. The spacecraft traveled some 4 billion miles (6.4 billion km), reaching speeds of nearly 37,282 mph (60,000 kph) to get alongside comet 67P/C-G in September 2014.

A BUMPY LANDING

Flying just 12 miles (20 km) above the comet's surface, a landing site was carefully picked out. *Rosetta* carried a small landing probe called *Philae*, which was about the size of a large washing machine. On November 12, 2014, *Philae* was released on a seven-hour descent onto the comet's surface.

The landing was not smooth. The harpoons that were supposed to anchor *Philae* to the comet's surface failed to fire, and the little probe ended up bouncing off the comet twice before finally coming to rest in a dark cave-like structure.

THE END

Left unexpectedly in a dark place and without solar power, *Philae's* main battery drained out in less than three days. It still managed to send back amazing pictures of the comet's surface and measurements of the temperature changes. On September 30, 2016, the *Rosetta* spacecraft was sent on a collision course with comet 67P/C-G.

Inspired by this mission, plans are being made to return to comet 67P/C-G to collect rock and dust samples from its surface for study on Earth.

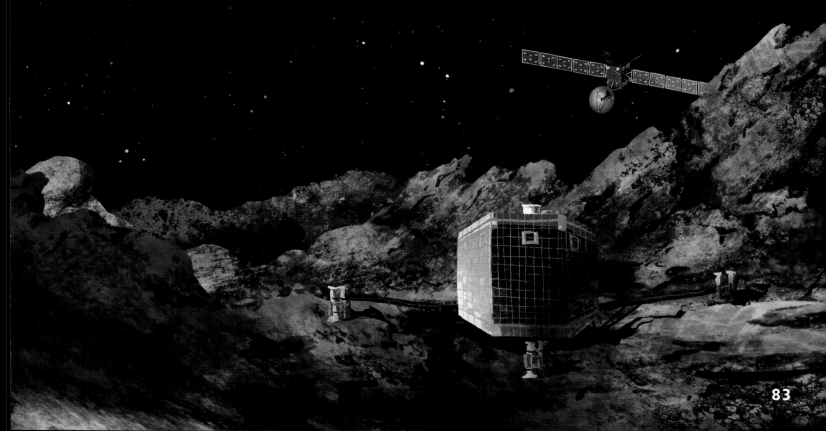

NEW ROCKET SCIENCE

The distances in space are enormous, and it takes many years for spacecraft to reach planets across the solar system. Leaving our solar system to explore other stars and their planets is even more difficult. Scientists are working on new and advanced technologies that could make our spacecraft go faster and farther. Let's take a look at some of the new rockets we can look forward to in the future.

SOLAR SAILS

On Earth we are used to seeing air particles (or wind) blowing onto large sails to propel boats across seas and oceans. In space, it is possible to use the energy of light to push on giant sails attached to spacecraft. Light is made of particles called photons, and the energy carried by the photons can drive forward the solar sails. The sails have to be very large and extremely thin. Spacecraft powered by solar sails could gently pick up speed and travel much faster than normal rocket fuel spacecraft. Scientists believe solar sails could be made large enough, perhaps longer than 50 soccer fields, and made to pick up speeds of nearly 10 percent of the speed of light, which is more than 62 million mph (100 million kph)!

FISSION ROCKETS

The nucleus of an atom is made up of particles called electrons and protons. Some nuclei can be split into smaller nuclei by smashing other particles known as neutrons into them. This is called nuclear fission, and it can release a huge amount of energy—on Earth we use fission to make electricity in nuclear power plants. Spacecraft of the future could also be powered by nuclear fission engines that push them to greater speeds. A fission rocket could shorten the flight from Earth to Mars from around seven months to three months, making the journey much easier for our astronauts.

ION PROPULSION

Another type of new engine that allows spacecraft to travel faster is called an ion drive. This engine works slowly, pushing the craft to pick up speed gradually over months and years. The ion engine shoots out gases much faster than the jet of a chemical rocket. The ions are electrically charged atoms pumped out from powerful electric guns. The *BebiColombo* mission to Mercury (*see pp. 74–75*) is using an ion engine to speed it on its way.

STARS

For many thousands of years, humans have watched and wondered about the stars in the sky. Our ancestors worshipped the stars and featured them in stories and myths. On any clear night, stars are the most fascinating objects you see with the naked eye, and although they may look like tiny points of light, they are in fact huge balls of very hot gas. They only appear so tiny because they are so far away.

Stars are the building blocks of the universe, and grouped into their billions, they give galaxies their shape, light, and history. Stars create important elements such as carbon, nitrogen, and oxygen. The study of the birth, life, and death of stars is one of the most important areas of astronomy. The life stories of stars also tell us about how they affect their surroundings and the role they play in forming many objects, such as planets and black holes.

OUR STAR, THE SUN

The Sun is one of almost **200** billion stars in our Milky Way galaxy. It lies about 26,000 light-years away from the center of the galaxy, moving around in a vast orbit that takes **250** million years to complete! The Sun formed about **4.6** billion years ago out of an enormous rotating cloud of gas and dust known as the solar nebula.

Like all stars, the Sun is a giant ball of extremely hot gas. Hydrogen, the lightest of all the elements, makes up 72 percent of the Sun's mass, while helium accounts for about 26 percent. The surface of the Sun is 9,932 °F (5,500 °C), but the temperature in its center can reach 27 million °F (15 million °C).

RULER OF THE SOLAR SYSTEM

With its place at the center, the Sun is by far the largest object in the solar system. It contains 99.8 percent of the entire mass of the solar system, giving it a powerful gravity that holds all the planets in their orbits. Its diameter is 109 times that of Earth, which means that the space inside its ball shape could fit a million Earths! The heat and light from the Sun affects the atmospheres of all the planets, while also allowing life to thrive on Earth.

ACTIVITY

The surface of the Sun is constantly changing. Sometimes, dark circular patches called sunspots appear, which are cooler areas than the surrounding surface. The number of sunspots on view changes depending on how magnetically active the Sun is. The annual sunspot count increases and then decreases over an 11-year cycle.

Powerful explosions can also be seen on the Sun, such as violent eruptions called flares. Another spectacular event is called a coronal mass ejection (CME). A single CME can launch 22 billion tons (20 billion metric tons) of hot, electrified gas into space. If the ejected matter strikes the Earth, it can cause electrical storms in the atmosphere. We see these as colorful displays in the sky known as auroras.

MULTIPLE LAYERS

The interior of the Sun is made up of many layers. The innermost part at the center is the core, where the Sun's energy is generated. Above the core is a large layer where energy travels outward, called the radiative layer. The layer above that is called the convective layer, where large bubbles of hot gas are pushed upwards. The surface layer that we can see from Earth is the photosphere. All the light of the Sun emerges from the photosphere. Above the photosphere is a thin solar atmosphere known as the chromosphere. Finally, there's a very thin corona that is usually seen as ghostly, shimmering light during a total eclipse of the Sun.

NUCLEAR ENERGY

Stars are massive and contain huge amounts of gas that can be used to generate an enormous amount of energy, lasting for billions of years. Using our eyes alone, we can see the energy as light from stars that can be thousands of light-years away.

POWER OF THE SUN

The Sun and other stars are powered by nuclear fusion reactions. In a fusion reaction, two light nuclei of atoms are smashed together to make a heavier nucleus of another atom—and this reaction puts out a lot of energy. The nuclear fusion reactions happen in the center, or core, of a star, where temperatures can reach more than 27 million °F (15 million °C). In the core of the Sun, hydrogen nuclei are crunched together to make a helium nucleus, releasing energy in the form of light and tiny particles called neutrinos.

Today, the Sun is converting 771 million tons (700 million metric tons) of hydrogen into 766 million tons (695 million metric tons) of helium every second in nuclear fusion reactions. The energy produced in the core, in the form of light, keeps bouncing around for a long time inside the Sun. A single particle, or photon, of light can take up to 100,000 years to reach the surface and escape, which we then see as sunlight.

THE SUN AND EARTH CONNECTION

Our star, the Sun, is very important for almost everything on Earth. It provides the heat and energy for life to thrive—the heat from the Sun keeps liquid water on our planet's surface and provides energy for the water cycle. The Sun also controls our seasons and climate, while its strong gravity keeps the Earth and solar system together.

Earth's magnetic field

Solar winds

SPACE WEATHER

The environment in space around the Earth depends a lot on the Sun. This is known as space weather. Even though we are 93 million miles (150 million km) away, activity happening on the surface of the Sun can directly affect Earth. The Sun is always spewing out gas and electric particles into space in a stream of matter known as the solar wind. The Earth's magnetic field shields us from most of the harmful particles coming from the Sun, but sometimes, matter from the solar wind slams into our atmosphere and we get treated to beautiful glowing lights called auroras.

The activity on the Sun can get very strong and violent. Explosions known as flares can suddenly release huge amounts of energy. Another powerful solar eruption is known as a coronal mass ejection. The radiation and particles from these Sun storms can be harmful to astronauts and our communication satellites. Scientists use many different instruments to keep an eye on the space weather and how active the Sun is. They can then send alerts to keep astronauts safe and prevent damage to satellites.

THE BIRTH OF STARS

Peering into the night sky, we can pick out the sites where stars are being born. These stellar nurseries are known as nebulae. The Orion nebula in the constellation of Orion is a famous example. It lies about **1,350** light-years from us and has enough material to make thousands of new stars.

AN ACT OF GRAVITY

All stars are made of gas, and our galaxy has lots of it, mainly hydrogen and helium. The gas, along with tiny particles of dust, forms clouds that lie in a space between stars called the interstellar medium. Slowly, gravity pulls this matter together and squeezes it into a smaller space, and whenever gas is squeezed like this, it heats up. Because the cloud of gas and dust is also spinning, over many hundreds of thousands of years it flattens into a platelike shape known as a disk. At its center is a superdense and superhot ball of gas. Under the crush of gravity, this central ball reaches an incredible 27 million °F (15 million °C). Stars in galaxies can vary greatly—some may have a mass of the Sun, while others can start their lives 100 times more massive.

BURST OF ENERGY

When the gas in the center of a baby star is squeezed tightly at a temperature of 27 million °F (15 million °C), it becomes possible for the atoms to fuse together to form helium atoms. Nuclear fusion occurs and the star is born and begins to shine brightly. A star like the Sun can make energy from this nuclear fusion fuel for 10 billion years.

LEFTOVERS

The enormous energy released at the birth of a star helps to blow away the surrounding gas and dust. Some of the material left over in the disk after the star has formed goes on to make planets, moons, comets, and asteroids. This is how we ended up with our full solar system.

A DEEPER LOOK

Since the birth of a star occurs deep in dust, we are not easily able to see what's going on. However, infrared light, which our eyes can't see, can travel through the dust clouds. Today, astronomers are using the powerful James Webb Space Telescope (*see pp. 32–33*) to detect the infrared glow coming from star-making factories in many nebulae across our galaxy and in other galaxies.

OUR STELLAR NEIGHBORS

There are more than 200 billion stars in our Milky Way galaxy, spread across a distance of 100,000 light-years. The light from most of the stars that we can see with our naked eye has traveled for more than 1,000 years to reach us. Coming closer in to a region of around 50 light-years around the Sun, we find about 1,800 stars. We think of this small patch of the cosmos as our local stellar neighborhood.

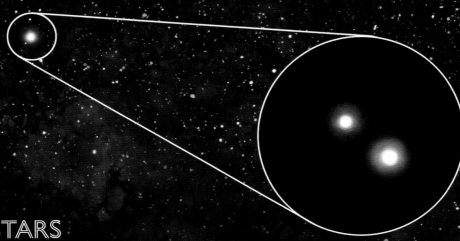

CENTAURI STARS

The closest star system to the Sun is a group of three stars called Proxima Centauri, Alpha Centauri A, and Alpha Centauri B. Proxima Centauri is the nearest star to us at about 4.2 light-years. This is still 25 trillion miles (40 trillion km) away! Alpha Centauri A and B orbit closely around each other in a pair know as a binary.

ROSS 128

A faint red star about a fifth of the size of the Sun, Ross 128 lies 11 light-years away in the constellation of Virgo. Most of this star's energy comes out in infrared light. It is about 9.5 billion years old, which is more than twice the age of the Sun. Astronomers think Ross 128 has an Earth-sized planet orbiting around it.

WOLF 359

In the constellation of Leo is another local star—Wolf 359. Located about 7.8 light-years away, Wolf 359 is one of the dimmest stars in our neighborhood. If we swapped our Sun with Wolf 359 in the center of the solar system, the daylight would be so dim that it would appear barely 10 times brighter than the full Moon we normally see at night.

CAPELLA SYSTEM

Toward the edge of our stellar neighborhood, about 42 light-years away, is a star system named Capella. It looks like one bright golden-yellow star in the night sky, but it's actually a system of four stars. Two of the Capella stars are about 10 times larger in diameter than the Sun, and together they put out 130 times more light than the Sun. The other two stars in the quadruple system are much smaller and cooler. These types of stars are called red dwarfs.

A ZOO OF STARS

Look carefully at the night sky, and you'll see that not all stars are the same, tiny pinpricks of light—some appear much brighter than others. Stars can also be different colors; some are yellow-white, while others shine with shades of red or blue.

Stars are not all born with the same mass or size, and they can have different life cycles from birth to death. When we gaze up at the night sky, we are seeing stars that are at many different phases in their lives, which is why there is such an amazing stellar zoo to look at. There are young stars, dwarfs, giants, supergiants, and strange dead stars in the cosmos.

BIG OR SMALL

Stars can range in size from squashed-up objects around the size of a city to swollen stars, large enough to swallow half our solar system! There are supergiant stars that can be more than 1,500 times larger than our Sun. Toward the end of their lives, a lot of star material can be packed into a small space by the force of gravity. A type of dying star called a white dwarf is similar in size to Earth. Even more tightly packed are neutron stars, which can be just 12 miles (20 km) in diameter.

BLUE OR RED

The color of a star will vary according to its surface temperature. The hotter stars are blue or blue-white. Their upper layers can be more than 54,000 °F (30,000 °C). The coolest stars are red, and their temperature is around 5,500 °F (3,000 °C). Our Sun has a temperature on its upper layers of about 10,800 °F (6,000 °C), and it glows white. Look for the amazing variety of stars when you next explore the night sky—there's a jewel box of colorful wonders up there!

BRIGHT OR DIM

There are two main reasons why stars may appear either bright or dim to your eyes. The first is distance. The Sun appears very bright in the sky because it is very near to us at a distance of 93 million miles (150 million km). We see the stars in the night sky as faint specks of light, because they are many light-years away from the Earth.

Some stars appear brighter because they give out enormous amounts of energy. A hypergiant star named the Pistol Star puts out 10 million times the power of the Sun. We still can't see the Pistol Star with just our eyes though, because it is 25,000 light-years away.

LIFE AND TIMES
OF THE SUN

The life story of the Sun will be acted out over **10** billion years or so. It will spend most of its lifetime fusing hydrogen to helium and releasing energy to keep itself shining steadily. Astronomers believe the Sun's fuel tank is now half empty, and that the remaining hydrogen in the core will be used up within another **5** billion years. The Sun's stability and appearance will then start to change quickly.

RED GIANT COMING

With the central solar engine no longer providing energy, the gravity of the vast ball of gas will gain the upper hand and start to transform the star. The Sun will be in crisis. Through many swellings, the Sun will bloat outward until its radius is about 30 times greater than it is today. This phase in the life of all Sun-like stars is known as a red giant. There are numerous examples of stars that have already reached this retirement age, such as Arcturus in the constellation of Bootes and Aldebaran in Taurus.

SCORCHED EARTH

The ballooning of the Sun into a red giant raises a question—how will this affect the Earth? The slow demise of the Sun over the next 5 billion years will be bad news for the Earth and its neighboring rocky planets.

A large red giant Sun will cause the temperature of the Earth to rise, and water will evaporate from the oceans. A few billion years from now, the temperature on our planet could reach close to 212 °F (100 °C)! All life, including the hardiest microbes, will have died out. Enormous volcanoes will spew gases into a rainless atmosphere, while a strong greenhouse effect will raise the temperature further to a sizzling 482 °F (250 °C). About 2 billion years later, the Sun will have expanded out to a radius of almost 105 million miles (170 million km). The innermost planet, Mercury, will be rapidly swallowed. Venus is also predicted not to escape the solar swelling and will find itself nearly 19 million miles (30 million km) below the red giant Sun's surface. It may be that the orbit of Earth will move outward, and our planet could narrowly escape the reach of the fully bloated Sun. Even if Earth escapes being gobbled up, the red giant Sun will appear huge and cover almost half the sky!

A STUNNING END

After the red giant stage, the outer layers of the Sun will get puffed out into space like giant smoke rings. Over a period of 10,000 years or so, these layers of gas will spread over vast distances, forming a colorful object known as a planetary nebula. Almost 1,500 planetary nebulae have been discovered so far in our Milky Way galaxy. One of the nearest lies about 650 light-years away in the direction of the constellation of Aquarius. Known as the Helix Nebula, the ejected outer layers of the dying star are seen in vivid colors. The main rings of matter in the Helix Nebula span a diameter of almost 1.5 light-years and were formed between 6,000 and 12,000 years ago. Another good example of a planetary nebula is the Cat's Eye Nebula, seen toward the constellation of Draco.

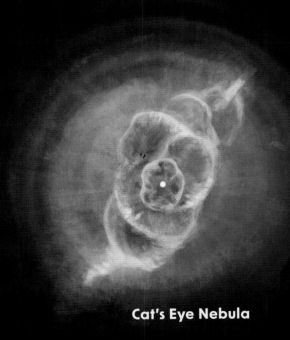

Cat's Eye Nebula

THE FINAL ACT

Over the course of around 20,000 years, the light from our Sun's planetary nebula will fade away as the expelled gases expand, cool, and scatter into the space between the stars. The object left behind will be a core of highly squeezed carbon known as a white dwarf star. This is where the story of the Sun's life finally ends. Having been squeezed into a planet-sized ball, the initially very hot cinder will gradually cool. Over billions of years, the Sun will then slowly turn from a hot

THE MOST MASSIVE STARS

The Sun may be the most massive object in the solar system, but on a scale of other stars, it is really very average. There are stars in our galaxy and other galaxies that are born with masses more than **100** times that of the Sun. These massive stars have powerful affects in galaxies. They have much shorter lives than our Sun and end their existence in dramatic supernova explosions.

BORN HEAVY

One of the most massive stars is called R136a1. It lies about 163,000 light-years away in a neighboring galaxy known as the Large Magellanic Cloud. R136a1 has a mass of 315 times the Sun—that is almost 100 million times heavier than Earth! This massive star is aging so fast that although it is only a million years old, it's already middle-aged. R136a1 is not only massive, but also vast, with a radius 30 times that of the Sun.

**From largest to smallest:
R136a1; a blue giant;
the Sun; a red dwarf**

GREAT POWER

Massive stars can have surface temperatures as high as 360,000 °F (200,000 °C) and emit a lot of light and radiation. This energy can warm up cold clouds of gas that surround the stars, making them glow when viewed through a telescope. Massive stars have stellar winds—flows of gases and particles ejected from the upper atmospheres of stars—that are much more powerful than the solar wind. The Bubble Nebula surrounds a star 40 times more massive than the Sun.

THE FIRST STARS

Astronomers believe that the very first stars were formed when the universe was around just 100 million years old. These first stars may have been very massive, ranging between 20 to 300 times the mass of the Sun. They would have also been extremely hot and bright, shining with the energy of at least 1 million Suns.

The first stars born in the universe lived very short lives and we would need very powerful telescopes to look far enough back in time to see them. The James Webb Space Telescope (*see pp. 32–33*) allows us to see billions of light-years away, which means that we are looking billions of years back in time. Eventually, this huge telescope in space will give us spectacular views of the most ancient galaxies. With any luck, we'll then be able to get glimpses of the first generation of massive stars that formed within them.

LIFE CYCLES OF STARS

Stars are not everlasting objects that never change. All stars follow life cycles of millions or billions of years—they are born, they change slowly as they age, and finally they die. By studying different stars in the universe and understanding how stars work, astronomers are able to chart the different stages of a star's life.

BIRTH MASS MATTERS

A star's mass when it is born is the most important factor when it comes to determining its life cycle. The larger its mass, the shorter its life cycle—and the more explosive its death. Smaller stars with much less mass can last many billions of years. We can roughly divide stars into three main types by their mass: lightweight, middleweight, and heavyweight. Each of these star types has a different life cycle.

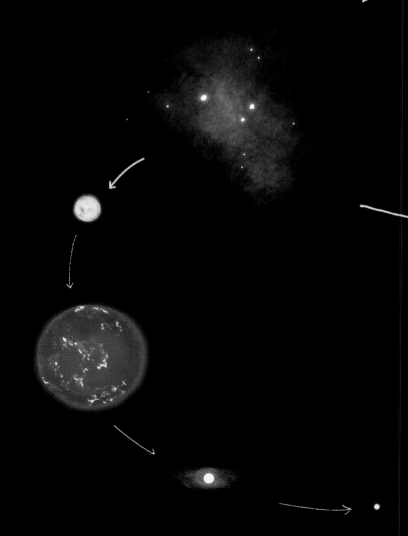

LIGHTWEIGHT STARS

Stars born with a mass about 0.5 to 8 times the mass of the Sun are lightweight stars. After their birth in a dusty cloud of gas (or nebula), lightweight stars shine steadily for about 10 billion years or so. The supply of hydrogen fuel in their core is then all used up, and no more nuclear reactions are possible to power them. They begin to change and move along the life cycle, first by swelling up into red giant stars and then by puffing out all the outer layers and becoming planetary nebulae. Lightweight stars end their lives as squashed-up stars called white dwarfs, which are about the size of Earth. The Sun is a lightweight star.

MIDDLEWEIGHT STARS

Stars born with about 8 to 20 times the mass of the Sun are middleweight. Their life cycles will be shorter than lightweight stars, perhaps only lasting a billion years or so. When all the nuclear fusion reactions in the cores of these stars come to an end, gravity collapses the outer layers down onto a core made of iron. The layers bounce off the core and get pushed out in a powerful, violent explosion called a supernova. Middleweight stars end their lives as city-sized objects called neutron stars.

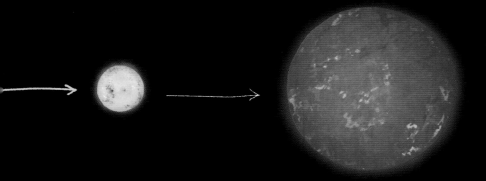

HEAVYWEIGHT STARS

The most massive stars are born with masses of more than 20 to 100 times that of the Sun. Their life cycles barely last a few million years. They use up all their supplies of nuclear fusion material and swell into enormous supergiant stars. Heavyweight stars have the most violent deaths, with extremely powerful supernova explosions ripping them apart. The very strange object left behind at the end of a heavyweight star's life cycle is called a black hole.

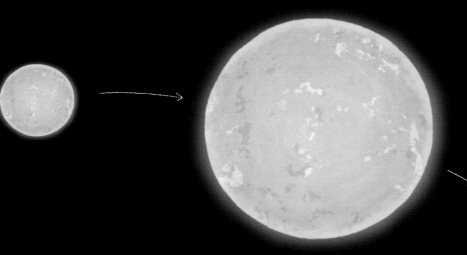

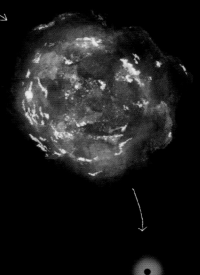

WHITE DWARF STARS

The way a star changes during its life cycle, and how it eventually dies, depends on the mass it had at birth (*see pp. 102–103*). The corpse left behind at the end of a lightweight star's life is known as a white dwarf. The vast majority of stars in the universe will end their existence as white dwarf stars.

EXTREMELY DENSE

Once all the nuclear fusion energy in Sun-like stars has been used up, the central core collapses down into a hot ball of mostly carbon and oxygen. Crushed by the force of gravity, matter that is almost the size of the Sun's mass is squeezed down into a ball the size of the Earth. This makes white dwarf stars among the densest objects in the universe. If you could bring a teaspoon worth of white dwarf material to Earth, it would weigh as much as an adult elephant!

Being so densely packed, a white dwarf star has a tremendous gravity pulling down on its surface. Its gravity is 350,000 times stronger than Earth's, which means that a person weighing 155 lb (70 kg) on Earth would weigh almost 55 million lb (25 million kg) on a white dwarf!

The nearest known white dwarf to Earth is called Sirius B. It is a tiny companion star of the brightest star in the night sky, Sirius. This pair are about 8.6 light-years from Earth. Our Sun is destined to become a white dwarf star in about 5 billion years.

Sirius B

Sirius

SHINING BRIGHT

When it first forms, a white dwarf can have a surface temperature of 180,000 °F (100,000 °C). Because of the energy stored in this heat, the white dwarf shines brightly. Slowly, this energy radiates away into space, and the star starts to cool and get dimmer. With the temperature dropping, the carbon and oxygen interior starts to become like crystal, turning the star into a diamond-like material! Over trillions of years, the white dwarf will cool completely and will eventually become a dead ball of dark matter called a black dwarf.

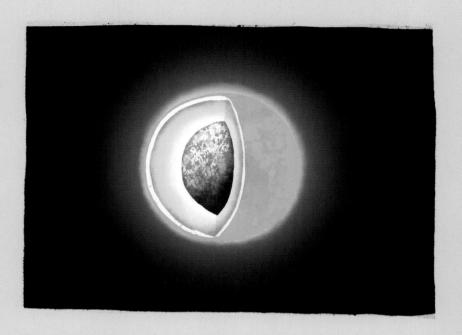

EXPLOSIVE PAIRING

Some white dwarf stars are one of a pair of stars known as a binary. In this case, if the two stars are very close to each other, matter can be pulled off the second star and dumped onto the surface of the white dwarf. If enough matter is transferred, the extra mass will cause the white dwarf to collapse. This can lead to a violent supernova explosion that destroys the white dwarf.

NEUTRON STARS

Neutron stars, the incredibly tightly packed remains of massive dead stars, are among the most mysterious and strangest objects in the universe. When a middleweight massive star erupts in a supernova explosion, it leaves behind its core. This object is called a neutron star.

TIGHTLY PACKED

A neutron star is a super-packed ball of neutrons, the tiny particles that make up the insides of almost all atoms. Gravity squeezes together neutrons nearly three times the mass of the Sun into a space that is just 12 miles (20 km) across! The particles are so squashed that one sugar cube's worth of neutron star matter would weigh around a billion tons on the Earth—that is almost as much as a mountain!

MEGA GRAVITY

Squeezing a huge amount of material into such a tiny space makes the pull of gravity very strong. In the case of a neutron star, its gravity is 200 billion times stronger than the gravity on Earth. The gravity is so crushing that if you were unfortunate enough to be standing on a neutron star, the downward pull of its gravity would totally flatten you into a very thin layer of particles!

PULSARS

Since neutron stars are tiny and dead, they don't put out light that we can easily see. There is, however, a type of neutron star that we can pick out. When a massive star is crushed down in a supernova explosion, it starts to spin very fast. Some neutron stars spin 40,000 times every minute. You can compare this to the Earth, which turns once on its axis every 24 hours! When a neutron star spins this fast, it creates a very strong magnetic field, which can beam out pulses of radio waves. This type of neutron star is called a pulsar, and we can detect them using radio telescopes on Earth.

THE CRAB NEBULA

In 1054, Chinese astronomers recorded the explosion of a massive star in the constellation of Taurus, some 6,000 light-years away from Earth. We see the leftover hot gas from this explosion as an object called the Crab Nebula. The center of the Crab Nebula is home to a fast spinning pulsar—a ball of neutrons just 12 miles (20 km) in diameter—turning 30 times every second. The strong magnetic field from the pulsar is ripping particles off the star and shooting them out as beams of energy.

BLACK HOLES

Our universe is full of strange and fascinating things, but black holes will truly stretch your imagination! A black hole is a tiny patch of space where the pull of gravity is so strong that even light cannot get out. As no light can escape a black hole, it appears invisible, or black.

FROM STARS AND GALAXIES

Black holes come in a variety of masses. A common type of black hole is made at the end of heavyweight star's life cycle (see pp. 102–103). When the dying star no longer has enough energy to push back against gravity, the huge star falls in upon itself. The force of the blow is so great, it causes a powerful supernova explosion, and a black hole is formed. Black holes made at the death of massive stars may be up to 20 times the mass of the Sun. There are also more massive black holes made in the center of galaxies, some of which are made when two galaxies smash into each other. These supermassive black holes can be many millions of times the mass of the Sun.

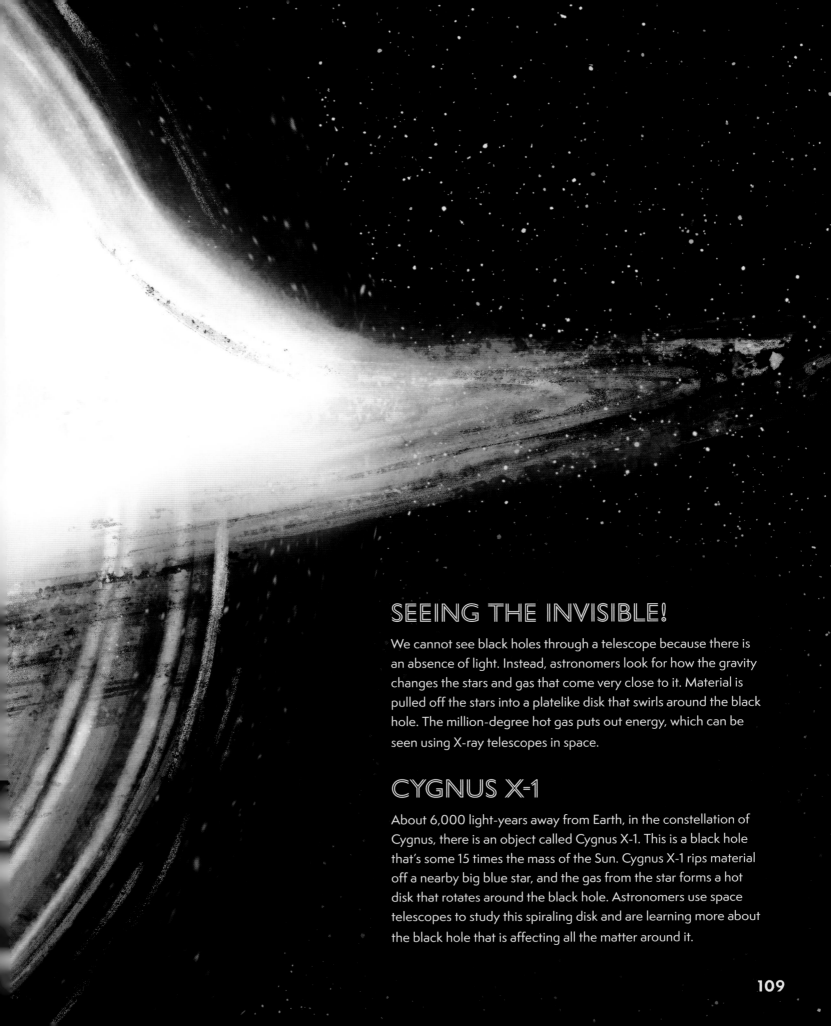

SEEING THE INVISIBLE!

We cannot see black holes through a telescope because there is an absence of light. Instead, astronomers look for how the gravity changes the stars and gas that come very close to it. Material is pulled off the stars into a platelike disk that swirls around the black hole. The million-degree hot gas puts out energy, which can be seen using X-ray telescopes in space.

CYGNUS X-1

About 6,000 light-years away from Earth, in the constellation of Cygnus, there is an object called Cygnus X-1. This is a black hole that's some 15 times the mass of the Sun. Cygnus X-1 rips material off a nearby big blue star, and the gas from the star forms a hot disk that rotates around the black hole. Astronomers use space telescopes to study this spiraling disk and are learning more about the black hole that is affecting all the matter around it.

RECYCLING
STARDUST

There's an amazing recycling process that takes place in
space as part of the life stories of stars. The planets
in our solar system, and even stars like the Sun,
would not exist without this cosmic recycling.
Over billions of years, chemical elements
are turned over several times to make
material that was used for oceans and
life on our planet.

1. STAR FACTORIES

The cycle starts with huge clouds of gas
and dust called nebulae. These are the
sites where stars are made, using mainly
lots of hydrogen and helium gas. The Orion
Nebula is an example of a star-making
factory in our Milky Way galaxy.

2. STAR LIFE

Once a star is born, it spends millions or billions of
years slowly releasing the energy from nuclear fusion
reactions. This energy makes the stars shine. The reactions
happen in the very hot centers of stars, making elements such
as carbon, oxygen, silicon, and iron. These elements, which are
heavier than hydrogen and helium, can only be made inside stars.

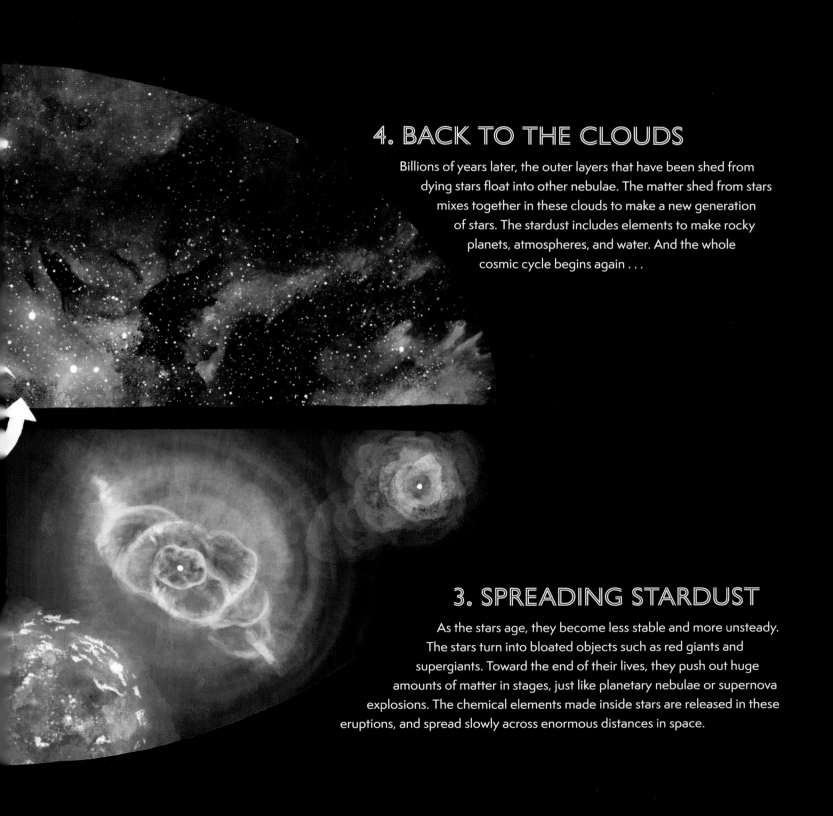

4. BACK TO THE CLOUDS

Billions of years later, the outer layers that have been shed from dying stars float into other nebulae. The matter shed from stars mixes together in these clouds to make a new generation of stars. The stardust includes elements to make rocky planets, atmospheres, and water. And the whole cosmic cycle begins again . . .

3. SPREADING STARDUST

As the stars age, they become less stable and more unsteady. The stars turn into bloated objects such as red giants and supergiants. Toward the end of their lives, they push out huge amounts of matter in stages, just like planetary nebulae or supernova explosions. The chemical elements made inside stars are released in these eruptions, and spread slowly across enormous distances in space.

A UNIVERSE OF GALAXIES

The universe is awash with more than 200 billion galaxies that we can see. These galaxies come in a huge range of shapes, sizes, masses, and energy, and together they make up the basic building blocks of the universe.

The galaxies are not evenly spread out in space. Pulled by the force of gravity, they swarm together to form galaxy groups, or clusters. Our Milky Way galaxy is a member of a group of over 40 galaxies. This collection is known as the Local Group, and it's part of a much larger gathering of at least 2,000 galaxies. They are tied by gravity into a cluster known as Virgo. In turn, the Virgo cluster is part of an even bigger supercluster known as Laniakea, which contains at least 100,000 galaxies! And this is just one of many other superclusters in the universe.

The clusters and superclusters form
a great spiderweb-like structure
over enormous distances in space.
This web makes up the grand
design of the universe.

OUR MILKY WAY GALAXY

Our home galaxy is called the Milky Way. It is a huge collection of hundreds of billions of stars and vast amounts of gas and dust, all held together by the force of gravity. If you could view the Milky Way galaxy from high above, it would look like a spinning pinwheel with spiral-shaped arms coming out from its center. But, since we are within the galaxy, we see it as a milky band of light in our night sky.

SCALE MODELS

End to end, the Milky Way galaxy is about 100,000 light-years across. The Sun and our solar system are not in the center—they lie about 26,000 light-years from the core, along a structure known as the Orion arm.

In order to grasp the size of our galaxy, imagine the Sun as a penny coin. If the Sun were that size, the nearest star, Alpha Centauri, would be about 348 miles (560 km) away. On this scale, the Milky Way galaxy would be nearly 8 million miles (13 million km) across. That's about 30 times the distance between the Earth and the Moon!

The galaxy is vast, but it has a mostly flat shape. Imagine placing two fried eggs back-to-back, with the yolks creating a central bulge—that's roughly the shape of the main galaxy.

**Earth's location
in the Milky Way**

Center of the Milky Way galaxy

Sagittarius A*

POWERFUL CENTER

The center of our galaxy lies toward the constellation of Sagittarius in the night sky. This region of our Milky Way galaxy is a really fascinating place. It contains very powerful objects, along with superhot gas. Some of the most massive stars known are found toward the center of our galaxy.

We can't easily see the center of the Milky Way since our view is blocked by dust, gas, and stars. But telescopes that can see in infrared light have revealed that a "monster" lies at the very core of our galaxy—a supermassive black hole named Sagittarius A* with a mass of more than 4 million Suns!

A STRANGE HALO

Our entire, flattened galaxy is surrounded by a huge ball-like shell known as a halo. Some of the oldest stars are found here, grouped into objects called globular clusters. Between 100,000 to 1 million stars can live in a single globular cluster.

Astronomers have discovered that the halo also contains large amounts of a strange and mysterious form of matter known as dark matter. We still don't know exactly what dark matter is, nor can we see it in telescopes. But we do know it is there because of the gravitational pull it has on nearby stars.

OUR GALACTIC NEIGHBORHOOD

The Milky Way galaxy is a part of a "neighborhood" of galaxies called the Local Group. It is made up of at least 40 distinct galaxies spread over a diameter of about 10 million light-years. There are many small or dwarf galaxies within this group, but our neighbors also include two other large galaxies aside from our own.

ANDROMEDA

The Andromeda galaxy is the closest large spiral-shaped galaxy to ours. Even though it is 2.5 million light-years away, the Andromeda galaxy is the most distant object humans can see with their eyes alone. Andromeda, also known as Messier 31, is about 200,000 light-years across. It has at least two spiral arms and a supermassive black hole hidden at its core. Almost 450 star-packed globular clusters are present in the outer halo of Andromeda.

Andromeda galaxy

Andromeda constellation

TRIANGULUM

Another large neighbor of the Milky Way is the Triangulum galaxy. It lies about 2.7 million light-years away toward the constellation of Triangulum. We can clearly see the spiral, pinwheel shape of this galaxy because it is face-on to us. It has a diameter of 60,000 light-years and contains 40 billion stars. The Andromeda and Triangulum galaxies are thought to be orbiting each other, locked together by gravity.

THE LARGE AND SMALL MAGELLANIC CLOUDS

Two of the nearest galaxies in our cosmic neighborhood are the Large Magellanic Cloud (LMC) and Small Magellanic Cloud (SMC). Both of these galaxies are less than 200,000 light-years away from us, and each contains a few hundred million stars. From the southern hemisphere, you can see the two galaxies as faint fuzzy patches in the night sky. They are orbiting our Milky Way galaxy, as well as each other.

The LMC and SMC have messy shapes. Thousands of new stars are being born inside them each year—some of the most massive and powerful stars known live in these neighbors of ours.

TYPES OF GALAXIES

There are likely trillions of galaxies in the universe, and they come in a range of sizes, shapes, masses, and ages. Some of these galaxies contain more than a trillion stars, while others may have as few as 100 million. Astronomers have grouped galaxies into four main types according to their shape: ellipticals, spirals, irregulars, and dwarfs.

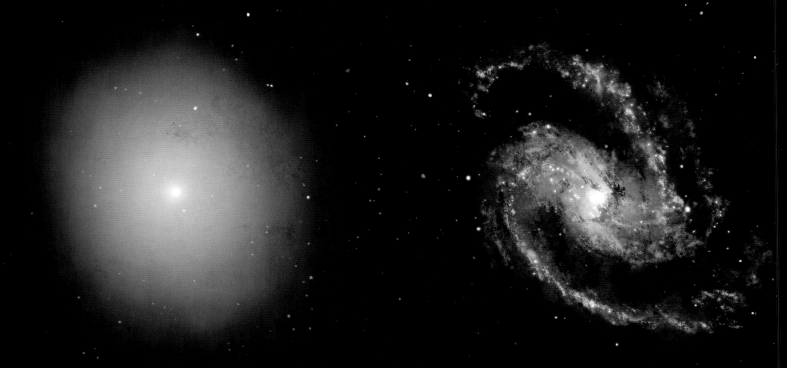

ELLIPTICALS

Some of the largest known galaxies are ellipticals. They can appear almost circular or egg-shaped, and they are made up of very old stars. IC1101 is a giant elliptical that lies about 1.1 billion light-years away from Earth in the constellation of Virgo. It is about 6 million light-years across, made up of more than 100 trillion stars, and is 2,000 times more massive than our Milky Way galaxy. Astronomers believe that large elliptical galaxies grow by swallowing up smaller galaxies.

SPIRALS

Spiral-shaped galaxies, such as the Milky Way or Andromeda, are the most common type of galaxy. Almost three-quarters of all large galaxies in the universe are spirals. They usually appear as flat, blue-white collections of stars, with spiral arms looping out from the central part. Spiral galaxies have lots of young stars and plenty of gas and dust to make new ones. Most of the stars in a spiral galaxy are found in an egg-like bulge at the center.

IRREGULARS

Some galaxies have a very messy appearance, with no clearly defined shape. These are called irregulars. Our neighbors, the Large Magellanic Cloud and the Small Magellanic Cloud, are examples of irregular galaxies. This type of galaxy is usually faint and only a few thousand light-years across.

DWARF

Unlike large spiral and elliptical galaxies that can contain hundreds of billions of stars, dwarf galaxies only have a few billion stars. Since this type of galaxy is very faint and small, astronomers do not know exactly how many of them are hidden away at great distances in the universe.

Many large galaxies are thought to have been built up by dwarf galaxies coming together and merging under the force of gravity. Astronomers study dwarf galaxies because they can teach us about how other galaxies have grown and changed over time.

OTHER GALAXY TYPES

Aside from the four main types of galaxies, there are some other unusual ones, including Seyferts, quasars, and lenticulars. Some have emerged from collisions between galaxies, while others are very powerful, with lots of action happening around supermassive black holes at their centers.

BUILDING A GALAXY

Shortly after the big bang, when the universe was still very young, there were no galaxies. Today, almost **14** billion years later, there are trillions of them. To understand how and when galaxies formed, astronomers use very powerful telescopes to look back in time to when the first stars were born. This is possible because light takes time to travel to us, so when we look at a very distant galaxy in our telescopes, we are seeing it as it was in the past.

FROM SMALL TO LARGE

The first structures to form after the big bang were small clumps of matter. Squeezed by gravity, they became knots of the first massive stars of the universe. The gravities of these knots pulled them together, creating much larger spinning objects. Slowly, more and more of these star-packed structures came together and created large galaxies, loaded with many billions of stars. It is possible that the most packed and densest clumps within galaxies collapsed under gravity and became black holes. And these, too, merged together to form supermassive black holes in the centers of galaxies.

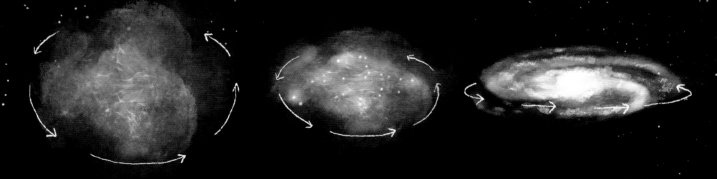

SLOW CHANGES

The shapes and makeup of galaxies change over billions of years. Galaxies are still forming today, while others are colliding and merging to make new galaxies. When a pair of a similar size smash into each other, they may become a single new giant elliptical galaxy. Some smaller galaxies, however, are ripped apart in collisions with larger galaxies. After billions of years, galaxies stop making new stars as they use up their supplies of cold gas and dust.

Laniakea supercluster

THE BIG PICTURE OF GALAXIES

Galaxies are not spread evenly across the universe. They are mostly bound together by gravity in small groups, which in turn are parts of much larger structures. If you could zoom out on a picture of the universe stretching billions of light years across, you'd see that the universe look like a vast cosmic spider's web!

CLUSTERS

Galaxy clusters are enormous objects that are held together by their own gravity. They contains hundreds or sometimes thousands of galaxies, along with very hot gas and a large amount of very mysterious stuff known as dark matter. The largest galaxies in the universe live in clusters.

COSMIC MAPS

Astronomers are using powerful 33-ft- (10-m-) wide telescopes on Earth to gather the light from hundreds of millions of galaxies. They are carrying out this huge survey in order to build a 3D map of the universe, stretching back more than 11 billion years. The measurements allow astronomers to work out the paths galaxies are flowing along. The 3D maps have revealed the largest structures in the universe.

Clusters of galaxies are collected to make up superclusters, and each supercluster contains chains of galaxy clusters. The largest superclusters span several million light-years in space. By mapping the universe, astronomers have shown that the galaxies are spread in threads, sheets, and walls. The space between these structures is almost empty.

OUR PLACE IN THE UNIVERSE

If somebody living in a distant galaxy wanted to post us an intergalactic package, what address would they need to send it to? The full "cosmic address" for Earth would be: Planet Earth, Solar System, Local Interstellar Cloud, Orion Arm, Milky Way, Local Galaxy Group, Virgo Supercluster, Laniakea Supercluster, the Universe!

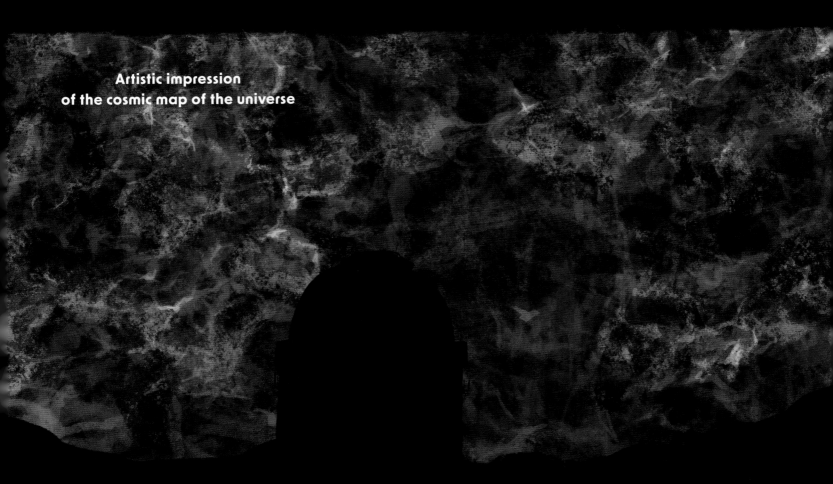

Artistic impression of the cosmic map of the universe

THE MOST POWERFUL GALAXIES

When the universe was very young, there were very powerful types of galaxies that put out at least **100** times more light than our Milky Way galaxy does today. These turbocharged galaxies are called quasars. We know of about a million quasars so far. We also know that their energy helped to shape the history of the universe.

FEEDING A SUPERMASSIVE BLACK HOLE

The great power behind quasars comes from their supermassive black holes, which can be between a few million to a billion times the mass of the Sun. These central monsters drag huge amounts of gas into the cores of the quasars, creating a raging whirlpool around the black holes. Moving at incredible speeds, the energy and motion of this matter creates enormous heat. Astronomers can detect this hot glow as many forms of light, such as radio waves and X-rays. Some quasars can burn up almost a thousand Suns' worth of matter every year!

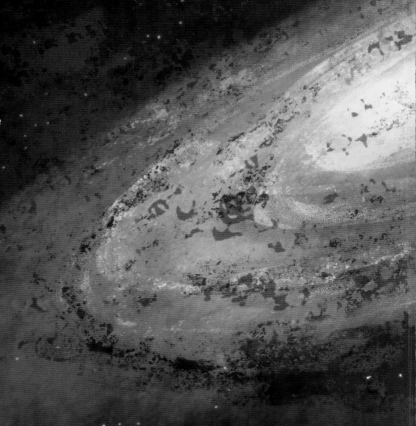

RECORD-BREAKERS

There are some truly record-breaking quasars. The brightest quasar ever seen in the early universe gives out the same amount of light as 600 trillion Suns. We can't easily see it, however, since it is so far away. The light we receive from this quasar started its journey into our telescopes when the universe was only about a billion years old.

POWER JETS

The spinning platelike material around supermassive black holes can also launch amazing jets of radiation and particles. These jets are incredibly powerful and contain particles that travel at near light speed. They often stretch well away from the quasars, smashing into matter that lies in the space between galaxies.

One of the longest jets in the universe is being spewed out by a quasar named PJ352-15. Using X-ray telescopes in space, jets of particles have been seen from this quasar that zoom out across 160,000 light-years. That's wider than the Milky Way galaxy!

SUPERMASSIVE BLACK HOLES

Astronomers believe that most galaxies, including our own Milky Way, have supermassive black holes at their centers. They are called supermassive because they contain millions or billions of times the mass of the Sun. While the black hole at the center of our galaxy has a mass of **4.6** million Suns, there are far more massive monsters out there! A galaxy called TON 618 is thought to host a supermassive black hole that is nearly **70** billion times the mass of the Sun.

HOW DID THEY GET THERE?

We are not sure how supermassive black holes are made. It is possible that they form when huge clouds of gas and dust are squeezed together by the force of gravity when the galaxy itself is forming. Another idea is that black holes created at the ends of the lives of massive stars grow over millions of years by gobbling up lots of surrounding material. It could also be that, early in the life of a galaxy, groups of many smaller black holes come together to form a supermassive one.

FINDING THEM

Black holes don't emit visible light that can be seen through normal telescopes. So how do we find them? The trick is to look for them in other forms of light coming from the material closely surrounding the black holes. Swirling whirlpools of gas and dust surround and feed black holes. The particles in their whirlpools move at great speeds, smash into each other, and heat up to temperatures of millions of degrees Fahrenheit. This very hot gas puts out radio waves, X-rays, and gamma radiation. Only by using special telescopes that can detect this radiation can astronomers study supermassive black holes.

GALAXY CRASHES

One of the most spectacular events in the universe is when two galaxies, each one loaded with billions of stars, get pulled together by gravity and collide. Many large galaxies can attract and swallow up smaller galaxies. Sometimes, two large galaxies of the same size will slam together to make a new supergalaxy, perhaps with their supermassive black holes combining. These galaxy crashes and mergers aren't quick—they happen very slowly over a few billion years. Excitingly, we are able to look across the skies and see some crashes in the making.

WHEN GALAXIES COLLIDE

Galaxies are mostly made up of stars and gas. When two spiral galaxies collide, it's very unlikely that the stars will smash together. This is due to the fact that, compared to their sizes, there is a great deal of space between the stars.

The gas in a galaxy, however, is much more spread out, forming giant clouds. The clouds don't miss each other like stars tend to do during a galaxy collision. The gas clouds can smash together with great force, which causes matter to clump together, creating new stars.

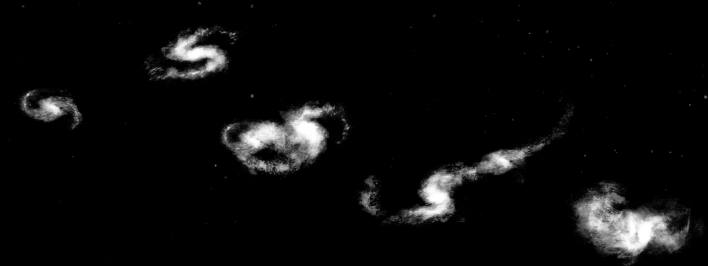

Pairs of galaxies can pass through each other several times during a collision, almost in a cosmic dance! On each pass, long streams of stars and gas can be pulled away, creating bridges between the galaxies. Gravity finally forces them to settle into a new galaxy.

THE GREAT SLAM TO COME

Astronomers have figured out that our Milky Way galaxy and the Andromeda spiral galaxy are heading toward each other. They are around 2.5 million light-years apart today and are getting closer—Andromeda is heading toward us at a speed of 248,000 mph (400,000 kph). At this rate, it will collide with our galaxy in around 4.5 billion years. The spiral structure of both galaxies will be destroyed, and we will likely end up with a new giant elliptical-shaped galaxy. The supermassive black holes of both galaxies will also merge. The gas consumed by the great new black hole could lead to powerful jets of matter, and the black hole could fling stars out of the new galaxy.

Many galaxies in the universe have had their shapes and content altered by galaxy crashes. This is an important step in the life and growth of galaxies.

THE EXPANDING UNIVERSE

The universe is getting larger and larger. In fact, it has been continually expanding since the big bang almost **14** billion years ago. Imagine it as a balloon being blown up. If you mark dots on the balloon to represent the galaxies, as the balloon gets larger, the dots will slowly move farther apart. When we picture the universe on the widest views, the galaxies are mostly moving away from each other.

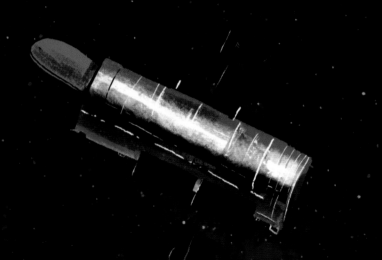

EDWIN HUBBLE

Our understanding of the universe today owes a lot to the observations of American astronomer Edwin Hubble. His work is so respected that he even has a telescope named after him! In 1929, while using telescopes at the Mount Wilson Observatory in California, USA, Hubble made the startling discovery that most galaxies are moving away from us.

Hubble's studies also showed us that the more distant the galaxy, the faster it is moving away, meaning that the universe must be expanding. His observations of the galaxies gave us the first theories on how our universe began with a big bang

ALONG FOR THE RIDE

The galaxies are moving away because space is stretching. The galaxies themselves are still held together by gravity and are not stretching or growing—it is only the space between galaxies that is getting larger. The galaxies are tagging along for the ride as space stretches!

RUNAWAY UNIVERSE

Astronomers have been measuring our distance to other galaxies in order to understand the growth of the universe. Using telescopes, they can spot explosions from supernova in distant galaxies. The brightness of these supernovae can be used to calculate how far away a galaxy is, and the speed at which it is moving away from us.

We had expected that the gravity from all the galaxies would pull back on the universe and slow down how quickly it was stretching. However, to everyone's amazement, the measurements showed us that the expansion of the universe had, in fact, sped up! The universe was expanding faster than it should be, suggesting that there must be an extra ingredient in the universe making this happen.

THE DARK SIDE OF THE UNIVERSE

The universe is a very mysterious place. Everything we have covered in this book so far—the planets, moons, stars, galaxies, gas, and dust—adds up to less than five percent of the universe! The other 95 percent is invisible and cannot be seen in our telescopes.

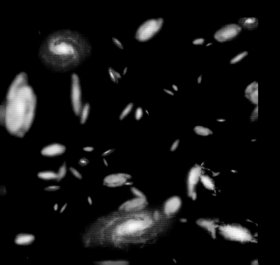

DARK MATTER

When astronomers studied galaxies, they noticed that the gravity of all the stars within them was not enough to hold everything together. Instead, with this amount of gravity, the stars should be flung out and scattered. Astronomers concluded that there must be something else inside and around the galaxies providing more gravity. This extra matter does not emit light, so we call it "dark matter."

About a quarter of the universe is made of dark matter. No one is sure what dark matter is actually made of, but it may be some unknown particle much smaller than an atom. There could be unimaginably huge amounts of these strange particles in the universe, and together their gravity acts to keep galaxies intact.

DARK ENERGY

We know that something mysterious is out there speeding up the growth of the universe, and that this rate of growth is getting faster and faster. This "something" is pushing space apart against the force of gravity and, it is winning! Astronomers call this new force "dark energy." Almost 68 percent of the universe is made up of dark energy.

We know even less about dark energy than we do about dark matter. We don't know what it is or where it comes from, but we can tell it's there. It may be an energy that's in empty space! So, as the universe expands and more space is created, even more of the weird energy appears.

Dark matter and dark energy together make up 95 percent of the universe. They are the biggest mysteries of the cosmos. Many scientists are studying galaxies and using mathematics to try and understand what this dark side of the universe is made of. There are great new discoveries to be made and so much more to learn!

WEIGHING
THE UNIVERSE

We have seen that the universe began about 13.8 billion years ago with a
big bang. It has existed ever since and continues to grow larger and larger.
Nobody is sure how the universe will change in the future
or whether it will ever come to an end, but many
scientists are exploring the universe to help
answer these questions.

MEASURING
IT UP

Many different measurements are
needed to help us understand the
fate of the universe. Astronomers
are using giant telescopes to map out
the movements of millions of galaxies.
They are also trying to figure out the
shape of the universe. Another important
measurement used is the mass of the whole
universe, but this is extremely difficult for us
to work out. You need to count not just the many
trillions of stars and galaxies, but also the mass from the
cold clouds of gas dust. Added to that is the amount of dark
matter and dark energy present in the universe.

AN ANCIENT GLOW

Astronomers are using satellites in space to study the leftover glow from the big bang. You can't see it with your eyes, but this glow appears all over the universe. The flash from the big bang is called the cosmic microwave background (CMB). Telescopes that can see in microwaves are used to detect this faint light.

Hot and cool spots, or patches, are seen in this earliest light from the universe. The spots tell us how much matter is packed into the universe and what type of matter it is. The cosmic radiation has shown that just five percent of matter is visible and is seen as stars and galaxies. Almost 27 percent is dark matter, and 68 percent is dark energy. All this would add up to an overall mass of the universe that is the same as 100 billion Milky Way galaxies!

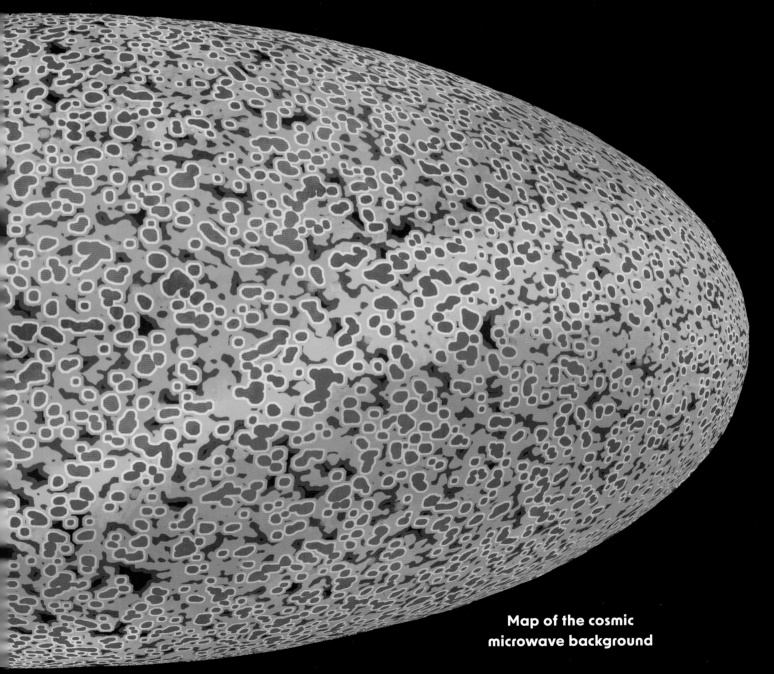

Map of the cosmic microwave background

THE BIG RIP

The universe had a beginning, and it will have an end. We are not sure how this end will come about, but we do know that dark energy will be involved. Dark energy is still one of the biggest mysteries of the universe—we don't know how it works or how it may change in the future. But we do know that the way the universe will end depends on how this dark energy works.

One possibility for the end of the universe is that it could tear itself to shreds! This is known as the big rip. Dark energy could be something so weird that it grows much more powerful in the future. The force of gravity holding objects in the universe together could ultimately be defeated by dark energy.

A big rip could occur when the expansion of the universe speeds up. Here, dark energy becomes so strong that instead of just moving galaxies away from each other, it rips them apart. In the end, the entire universe is destroyed. But don't worry— astronomers believe that if there is to be a big rip ending, it will not happen for many billions of years!

THE BIG CRUNCH

Another possible ending for the universe is known as the big crunch. Imagine now that this strange dark energy somehow gets weaker and less powerful in time. If this happens, gravity will start to have the upper hand and will pull objects, including entire galaxies, closer together. It's like gravity winning the tug-of-war over dark energy!

In the big crunch, the universe will slowly start to pull back on itself. It would shrink, become more tightly packed, and get much hotter. Stars, planets, and entire galaxies would clump closely together. In the end, the universe will very quickly crunch back in on itself—the very opposite of the big bang.

But instead of expanding and cooling, the universe will shrink and heat up. A hundred billion years from now, the universe would return to almost the same size as it was when the big bang first happened. Perhaps then, a force may kick in and start a new big bang cycle all over again!

THE BIG FREEZE

Many astronomers believe the most likely end to the universe is where dark energy stays as it is today—the universe just continues to expand gradually, while the space between galaxies slowly gets bigger. Over a very, very long time, the universe becomes emptier, darker, and much colder. This end of the universe is known as the big freeze, also sometimes called the heat death or the big chill.

SPREADING OUT OF SIGHT

In the big freeze, the universe becomes so vast that all the gas is spread very thin, and no new stars can form—gas needs to clump tightly together to make new stars. Over the next 100 trillion years, the universe becomes too cold for any life to be possible. All that remains are burned-out stars, cold, dead planets, and black holes. We will no longer be able to see any distant galaxies. The last stars in the universe will all begin to die, turning the lights of the universe off forever.

NOTHING LEFT

In the final stages of the big freeze, the atoms that make up matter will start to break apart and decay. All matter in the universe would slowly evaporate as a weak energy. Even black holes would break down, leaking away as a radiation. Finally, the universe will only exist as empty space and very feeble radiation. The big freeze is a universe that ends with nothing ever happening, since there is little or no energy left.

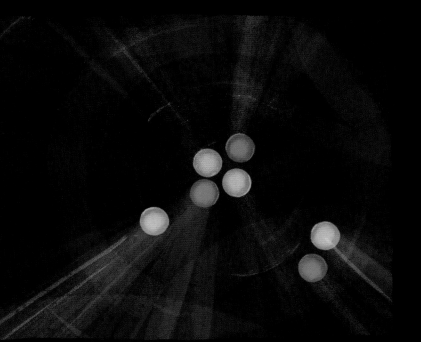

LIFE IN THE UNIVERSE

One of the most important questions we can ask is: "Are we alone in the universe?" Since the beginning of civilization, people have gazed into the night sky and wondered whether there is life beyond Earth. We have explored the whole cosmos in this book and have come across oceans on icy moons, planets orbiting around other stars, and trillions of galaxies. We have yet to find life of any kind anywhere else beyond Earth, but we are learning a lot more every day about what's in the universe. We have also built amazing new telescopes to continue the exciting hunt for life.

BIOSIGNATURES

Once an Earth-like exoplanet has been discovered orbiting a Sun-like star, scientists start looking for clues that suggest that the planet may support life. They are using powerful telescopes to study the atmospheres of exoplanets carefully, looking for substances produced by living things. These substances are called biosignatures, and they can be used to detect the presence of life.

On Earth, one of the most important biosignatures is oxygen, which is made in large amounts by the photosynthesis of plants and algae that grow here. An exoplanet with an atmosphere loaded with oxygen may be a sign that life flourishes there, too. Living things on other planets may produce ozone, ammonia, or methane gas, which could also be biosignatures.

LISTENING FOR ET!

For decades, astronomers have also been listening for signals possibly coming from intelligent life in the cosmos. They have been looking for radio messages from extraterrestrials (ET). Scientific studies that look for such signals are known as the Search for Extraterrestrial Intelligence (SETI). One such search, called Phoenix, was carried out between 1995 and 2004. Phoenix used radio telescopes to listen for signals from 1,000 nearby star systems within 150 light-years of Earth. Most of these stars were similar in size and brightness to the Sun.

In 2016, a new project called Breakthrough Listen started a 10-year-long survey of one million of our closest stars, using a 328-ft- (100-m-) wide radio telescope in West Virigina, USA. To help hunt through the huge amount of radio measurements being collected, members of the public are being invited to volunteer and use their own computers at home.

Perhaps somewhere beyond our Earth, life has taken root and is thriving. Who knows how that life will evolve and what path it will follow. And whether we will ever meet!

GLOSSARY

ATMOSPHERE A blanket of gases surrounding a planet or a moon.

ATOM A basic building block of the universe. Atoms are made up of particles called protons, electrons, and neutrons.

AXIS An imaginary line through the center of a planet or moon, around which the object turns.

CONSTELLATION A group of stars that appear to form a pattern when viewed from Earth.

COSMOS The universe as a whole.

CRATER A bowl-shaped hole made by an object from space hitting the surface of a planet or moon.

CRYSTALS Pieces of solid matter that take on a structure with a repeating pattern of flat surfaces. These flat surfaces reflect light and can make the pieces sparkle when looked at from different angles.

GALAXY A collection of stars, gas, and dust, held together by gravity.

GLACIER A large amount of ice formed in cold regions from compressed snow that moves very slowly down a slope or across land.

GLOBULAR CLUSTER A group of thousands of stars that are very tightly bound by the force of gravity into a ball-like shape.

GRAVITY A force that pulls objects toward one another. Objects with a larger mass will pull on objects that are smaller than them.

INFRARED Light of low energy that is invisible but can be felt as heat.

MAGNETIC FIELD The lines of force that surround a permanent magnet or moving electric particles.

MASS A measure of how much matter an object contains.

NEBULA A cloud of gas and dust where stars are born.

OBSERVATORY A building where a telescope or other scientific equipment is housed.

ORBIT The circling of an object in space, such as a star or planet, by another object.

PARTICLES A tiny amount, or small pieces, of something.

PULSAR A rapidly rotating neutron star. It releases short pulses of radio waves and other electromagnetic radiation.

RADIATION The energy or particles released from substances or explosions.

SATELLITE An object that circles a planet. This can be a moon or an artificial satellite launched for navigation and communication.

SERVICE MODULE Part of a spacecraft that provides power and other items to support astronauts, such as water, oxygen, and food.

SUPERNOVA A huge explosion that takes place at the end of some stars' life cycles.

VAPOR A liquid or a solid that has become a gas because of heat or a change in pressure.

VOLCANO An opening in a planet's surface through which hot liquid rock is thrown up.

INDEX